DARK CRAVING

A WATCHERS NOVELLA

BY

VERONICA WOLFF

Dark Craving/ Veronica Wolff
ISBN: 978-1-941035-00-9

Cover Design by The Theater of Marketing

For Sophie Littlefield and Rachael Herron,
who shone the light at the end of my tunnel.

Chapter One

Twelve months ago

"Tracer Ronan." The vampire Hugo De Rosas Alcántara stared at me over steepled fingers. His face was unmarred by age, features smoothed by that utter stillness borne of immortality. To him, I was merely a man. Worse, a young man. And he was trying to make me squirm.

He leaned closer, peering at me. Leather the color of ox's blood creaked beneath him. The office decor, like his posturing, meant to menace. Alcántara was ancient, but more than that, he was a ruler. A creature of power among the most powerful.

"Is this impatience I read on your face?" he asked finally.

Just let me get on with it, I thought. I despised my job and wanted it done. It was a godforsaken place, this *Eyja næturinnar*. This Isle of Night. Nothing but gray cliffs, bleak skies, hostile seas. And vampires.

"You young humans." His lips pursed with contempt. "Always so anxious, racing to your own deaths."

Young, he called me. An irony seeing as Alcántara looked no older than my nineteen years. To him, I was weak.

A bit of mortal ephemera. Flesh with an expiration date—one that he controlled.

"Not at all," I assured him. Mine was a game that went deeper than impatience and fear. The day would come when Alcántara learned how greatly he'd underestimated me. For now, though, I gave him a subservient nod. "I'm merely looking forward to getting on my way."

"On your way, is it?" He leaned back with a sneer. "You fashion yourself quite the lone wolf, don't you? A ma-ver-ick." He pronounced each syllable of the word slowly, disdainfully, his lips peeling back as he ended on the sharp, hard *k* sound, revealing a pair of long, gleaming fangs.

"No, indeed, Master Alcántara," I assured him in as formal a tone as I could manage. Let him think I was cowed.

"Best to remember, rebels are not tolerated." His mouth curved in a catlike smile. Lean and striking, sleek and dark, the Spanish vampire was a deadly panther in elegant human form. "You are merely a Tracer. *My* Tracer."

His Tracer. He believed this was all I might be. A human tool who brought unsuspecting adolescents to him—to their almost-certain deaths.

"Naturally." I thought I might've nodded in a gesture of respectful submission, but all I knew was the single thought driving me: One day this submission would end. One day I would destroy him. Slowly and with gusto.

Alcántara had immortality, power, and sway—and it meant he had everything to lose. Not me, though. I'd already lost everything. There was nothing left for me to fear. A sense of belonging, of hope and attachment. All those things that'd made me vulnerable had transformed into vengefulness the day he took my sister from me. The only family I've known, my Charlotte.

Gritting my teeth, I told him, "I have the names."

I despised the vampires—have always despised them—but I had to serve them. Each day Alcántara found me useful was another day I survived. Alive was good. I couldn't take them down if I were dead.

This mission would be like any other. The Vampire Directorate identified teenagers with the proper lineage, and it was up to me to assess them. For candidates to have even the slimmest chance of survival, they had to possess the correct blend of adverse emotion and experience. They had to be outsiders. Hostile. Neglected. There had to be resentment. Violence. And just the slightest glimmer of hope. I collected the teens who met these criteria and fetched them to this remote hell we called the Isle of Night. Here, the boys trained to be vampires and the girls to be Watchers—trained killers all of them, in the service of the Vampire Directorate. Few survived.

I'd lost count of the children I'd taken. I hated myself for it. But a part of me had stopped caring when Charlotte was killed. There was no longer anyone alive whose opinion I cared about. And one day, when I inevitably reached my limits, there would be nobody alive who'd mourn me as deeply as I now mourned my sister. It was my one comfort.

"Can you handle the assignment?" Alcántara asked. "I seem to recall your last mission ended with your charge floating facedown in the San Francisco Bay."

I bristled. He was referring to a male candidate—one of our Vampire Trainee recruits. I'd smuggled him out of juvie only to find he'd smuggled something out himself—a taste for meth and a homemade shiv he thought he'd use on me to get drugs. "He wasn't up to our usual standards."

"But leaving the child bobbing like a rotted fish for all the world to see?"

"I heard sirens," I explained, holding myself still in my seat. Vampires prized discretion at all costs. Tracers who ended up in police custody had very short life spans. "The authorities were too close. I had to act."

He tsk-tsked. "We try to be more discreet with our

refuse."

I thinned my lips in what I hoped approximated a penitent smile. "That won't happen again, Master Alcántara."

"It's the mistake of a young man. Perhaps you require more training to get your temper under control."

On the contrary, I prided myself on my control and professionalism, though I did let a little of it slip when I said, "Aye, I'm young, but I'm the best in the world at what I do."

I was his best, and he knew it. A well-trained Tracer could do a standard retrieval job in his sleep, and I was more than just a well-trained Tracer. I had a rare talent that made me more valuable than the others.

"I suppose you are the best," he admitted with a sigh. "For now. One day someone younger will come to take your place."

The threat wasn't a vague one. The job of Tracer didn't exactly come with a retirement package. I gathered my wits. "But I'm here now," I said, surprised when he laughed in reply. A cat testing the limits of his toy.

"You are here now," he agreed, "but not for long. You're off to gather two American girls. In Florida, is it?"

"Aye, Miami." Where the sun was so bright it bleached the sky to an intolerable glare and the air so thick with dampness it lingered in my sinuses and clung to my body like a mildewed cloak. "Bloody horrible place," I muttered before I thought to stop myself.

"I assure you," he snapped, "there is no need to be churlish. I can send Tracer Judge in your stead. A week chained in the caverns will give you plenty of time to contemplate the meaning of *bloody horrible place*."

"Apologies, Master Alcántara." I burned to destroy him and everything about this sick island, but for now, I bowed my head, blanking my features. I couldn't let him read treason on my face. "As ever, I appreciate your wise supervision."

"Indeed." He tilted his head with predatory consideration. "I believe it's precisely this guidance that's shaped you into such an able instrument."

He was reminding me of my place, and I reeled from a fresh wave of loathing. I had to get out of there. No longer able to stop myself, I shot a quick glance at the clock.

"You tire of our discussion?" Alcántara smiled, but I didn't mistake it for friendliness. There was no such thing as *friendliness* on this island. Friends were quick to die. Suspecting everything about everyone was what'd kept me alive so long.

"I don't want to miss my ferry." I resisted the urge to edge forward, to flee. "I leave for Oban at 18:30."

"A mere instant in time to we of the Vampire blood." He kicked back, casually crossing his black-booted ankles. He might've been hundreds of years old, but Alcántara looked like he'd be more at home in a New York nightclub than medieval Spain.

But then he froze. The door swung open, and his face hardened to marble.

A powerful presence hit my back like an invisible pulse of electricity.

"What is the meaning of this?" Alcántara demanded, his voice lethally sharp. Vampires prized things like order, custom, formality. Interruptions like this never happened.

I held my breath—I didn't dare turn to see who'd entered. Being challenged by a vampire was dangerous; watching one provoke another was surely a close second.

The feel of a savage force rippled over me, making my skin crawl. "There has been a change of plans," a ragged voice said, closing in.

A hand seized my shoulder. It was Master Alrik Dagursson; I recognized his bony, tapered fingers, more ancient claw than hand. I suppressed a shiver.

I angled my body to look up—it was unavoidable now—

and was met by a pair of eerily pale eyes, grotesquely round and deeply sunken into his cadaverous features. "Master Dagursson," I said in quiet, ceremonious greeting.

His only reply was a bored *hiss*, the smell of his breath something past decay, like a corpse left rotting to dust.

Long ago, vampires resolved to spend eternity surrounded by pretty things—young men and women, all of them clever, attractive, alluring—but Dagursson came from a generation before that. His was of a cruel time, one of Vikings and ice. An era before the affairs of the Vampire had evolved into remembrance and lore.

His eyes cut, fast as a snake's, from me to the Spaniard. "Hugo, I've added a third girl to the list."

"How peculiar"—the tension in Alcántara's voice hummed like a tuning fork—"Seeing as the list is not of your jurisdiction."

Alcántara was right. Generally my orders came from him alone, in this office. Only rarely did Dagursson emerge from his dusty lair, where he surrounded himself with ancient manuscripts and esoteric objects from bygone eras.

"I'm making it my jurisdiction," he snarled.

The temperature in the room dropped. Alcántara's alabaster features grew even paler, shimmering like ice. "Go back to your books, Alrik," he said, his words a cold, dangerously quiet whisper.

Dagursson made a show of considering then dismissing this, and then he returned his attention to me, his talon fingers digging deeper into my skin. "You are leaving soon. Can I trust you not to fail this time? I understand you left a body behind on your last assignment."

"I didn't fail," I said. I quickly regretted the hint of defensiveness in my tone. "That is to say, the candidate was no good."

Dagursson's pale eyes glimmered. "Self-justifying excuses are a failure for all of us." He removed his hand from my shoulder, slicing me with a razor-sharp fingernail. "But I will allow you to prove yourself"—he dropped a file in my lap—"with this."

"Alrik," Alcántara said in a low, level voice. "Perhaps you've forgotten: Tracers are my concern."

Dagursson's withered features hardened into something even more grotesque. "You are the one who's forgotten, Hugo. I am more senior than you."

I made my face utterly still so as not to betray my complete fascination. I'd never seen a vampire pissing contest before.

Alcántara's lips curled into a slow, considering smile. "You are older, it's true," he said in an oblique stab at the vampire's looks. "But when it comes to the job of Tracer and Acari, I wonder if you are wiser. You see, Alrik, while you spend your time with your archaic investigations"—despite being a scholar in his own right, Alcántara waved his hand dismissively at this—"I am focused almost exclusively on cultivating what has grown into a magnificent student body. I would that you not doubt me, my recruits, or the instrument I've chosen to retrieve them." He sat back then, feigning boredom. "Now perhaps you'll leave me to return to these relevant day-to-day decisions, and you can go back to poring over all those old papers you so—"

"I am the keeper of more than mere *papers*," Dagursson snapped. He glided to Alcántara's desk and unrolled a scroll. The crackle of paper as thin as onionskin spoke to how ancient it was. I caught a glimpse of handwriting, a blurred and cramped antique scrawl filling the page. There were lines branching into more lines—a family tree. He traced a finger down to a point then pinned the Spaniard with unwavering eyes. "It's time for the girl."

Confusion dawned into angry realization on Alcántara's face. "You wouldn't," he said sharply. "It's too soon. She's not ready."

"Or perhaps you're the one who's not ready." Dagursson stared at him for a long moment, impatience and challenge on his wizened face. "In fact, I believe you're dismissed."

"You can't dismiss me from my own office," Alcántara replied with quiet outrage.

I would've said the same. I'd thought the two vampires were peers, but this interaction told a very different story.

Alcántara scowled. Finally, in a voice like ice, he said, "As you wish, Alrik." And then he excused himself. From his own office.

In all my time, I'd never seen such a thing.

Dagursson perched formally on the sofa where Alcántara had been lounging just a moment before. "You claim I can trust your competence, Tracer, but can you handle retrieving a third girl?"

"Three isn't a problem," I said cautiously. It was an effort not to steal a glance at the door. I was still processing what'd just happened, wondering at the secret intrigue playing out before my eyes.

"Is it something you do often?" He leaned in, peering closer. "Retrieve that many?"

Does he really not know how this works?

"I've collected as many as five at once." I paused. There was a strange, taut feeling in the room, and it put me on guard. "Is there something more I should know?"

He met my question with another question. "What if one in your charge was too strong for your powers?"

An internal alarm went off, prickling the skin on the back of my neck. "That's never happened. These are children we're talking about."

The old Viking shrugged disdainfully. "You, too, are a child."

"I'm more powerful than that," I said with quiet certainty. I stopped being a child the day I was abandoned on this rock at the age of twelve.

"We'll see. This third girl is immature yet, but her strength might be more impressive than the norm. We must be cautious—none of us would be here had we not heeded every concern."

We. The Directorate.

"The file." He motioned to the dossier in my lap. "Read it. I expect you to memorize it." He gave me an impatient look. "*Now*, Tracer."

It began ordinarily enough:

Annelise Regan Drew (age 17)
Height: 5'2"
Weight: 120 lbs. (est.)
Hair: Blond
Eyes: Blue
State of residence: Florida
Education: High School (graduated 3.5 years)
Employment: tutor (various), entrepreneur (unauthorized sale of academic work), Fuddruckers restaurant franchise (cashier, prep, counter)

A pert blonde appeared in my mind's eye wearing a too-tight restaurant uniform, her skin taut and Florida-bronzed. "Americans," I muttered, "and their fetish for the ridiculous."

"Beware your preconceptions." Dagursson rose and walked to the fireplace, standing before it with the precise, erect posture that'd made him a shoo-in for the island's protocol and propriety classes. "I believe you'll find this candidate defies expectations." There was a glimmer of fang, a quick flash, part smile, part predatory anticipation.

Nodding, I turned my attention back to the file and reviewed details about her family—what few there were. "There are a lot of gaps," I said, noting the extensive passages that'd been blacked out.

Robert Buck "Bucky" Drew
Relation: Father
Priors: Two counts Misdemeanor Battery, Felony Battery [no conviction], Domestic Battery, Domestic Battery against a minor)
Employment: Titan Parts (SSI Disability pending)

It looked like her father had been a cruel drunk—it was a typical enough profile among our candidates—but her mother defied categorization. In fact, her description hadn't been much more than thick black lines obscuring biographical details.

{details redacted} Audunsson
Relation: Mother
{details redacted}
Employment: {redacted}
{redacted}

"It's…unusual." Generally these things read like police rap sheets, and yet the only person with any criminal history here was her father. "This is the candidate you thought might be too strong for me?" I asked in disbelief.

"If you have a point, speak it plainly," Dagursson ordered, "before I dispense with you and send another Tracer in your stead."

I gave an apologetic nod, too curious not to play along. "What I mean is, her environment and upbringing seem tough enough, but she's not…" I struggled for the exact way to put it. "She doesn't strike me as quite so hard-edged as our usual recruits. I mean, she spent"—I flipped back, finding the spot—"two years on her high school chess team." About as far from our typical profile as you could get. "Are you certain she wouldn't benefit from another year at home? We can arrange it so—"

"Young Tracer," Dagursson interrupted. "Perhaps the question is, are *you* certain? I confess, she reminds me of your Charlotte." He tsk-tsked in imitated sympathy.

Charlotte. Hearing the name was a punch in my gut. He thought this candidate was like my dead sister? I considered the details, and the two were nothing alike. Annelise was small and blond. Charlotte had been strong and dark. "I don't see the similarities."

He raised his brows, pointing to a note appended to the bottom of the page. "Perhaps not physically. But then there is the question of intellect…"

Psychogenic Profile

IQ classification: Superior

Cognitive, fluid, and standard intelligence quotient exams. (Deviation intelligence quotient and Stanford-Binet methodology.)

Subject's estimated IQ range: 175-190

So Annelise Drew was smart.

Lottie had also been bright—brighter than bright. It'd been her downfall. Though she'd never had any formal testing, my sister was always asking questions, burning to know more. She remembered everything, putting pieces together in a way that I saw now would've been a threat to those in charge. Because she didn't just want to learn everything, she wanted to *challenge* everything. Ceaselessly.

I schooled my features, imagining my cheeks were made of lead. My heart, too, was leaden. I must not lose focus. My wayward emotions had been what killed Lottie—I couldn't let them be the death of me, too. I purged all feeling from my voice as I said, "I suppose this candidate does seem quite smart."

"More than smart," Dagursson replied curtly. "What I speak of goes beyond a superior intellect. There is also a certain…insolence." He pursed his thin lips into a self-satisfied smirk. "Sarcasm. The word itself comes from the Greek *sarkazein*. Meaning 'to tear flesh.' Ironic, no?" With a wave of his hand, his face blanked once more into that gaunt, wrinkled mask. "Regardless, it's a modern sensibility that must be purged. Your sister had it also. It's why I've chosen you above the other Tracers. You, I believe, have the tools to manage her."

I'd believed Charlotte had simply been killed, bested in the fighting ring by another Acari. But Dagursson's implication was that more had been at work. It was too much to process, here, now, in front of this creature I so detested.

I needed to redirect. Suppressing my grief, I told him, "I will always remember my sister. But as I recall, we are speaking of this girl." I was gripping her file so hard the blood had leached from my fingertips. "Who is decidedly not Charlotte."

He gave a decisive clap to his hands. "And so you are right. It's this Annelise who's of special concern to us now." He leaned forward, his voice taking on a hard edge. "There is no *if* with this child. Whatever it takes, you will bring her to us. No matter the cost."

"Of course," I said. Fuddruckers and chess club. Easy enough quarry.

"I fear you haven't understood the full magnitude of this situation." His round, glassy eyes narrowed on me. "You will approach this mission as though your life depended on it…because it does." He spoke that last threat as though bored, and I knew his bored menace was what I should fear most.

I inclined my head gravely, speaking the words I knew he wanted to hear. "I won't fail you."

He waved this away impatiently. "Yes, yes, so I've heard. But Ronan? Simply retrieving her is not the end of it. Once Annelise Drew arrives, you will keep her alive."

My response was instant. "You know that's something I can't guarantee." Nothing on the island was a certainty, particularly not survival.

"Too true." Dagursson frowned. Paused. "Just as we cannot guarantee the safety of your family."

The pronouncement was Dagursson's hidden blade, and I felt it slice through my belly. Family of mine…and he knew how to find them. I dared not believe it.

I must've schooled my expression too well because Dagursson was quick to add, "You don't think I speak of your foster family, do you?" He sneered. "What need have we for a whisky-addled fisherman and a two-pence scullery? No, Tracer Ronan. I mean your blood kin." He peered down at me. "I see the doubt in your eyes, but doubt not, boy. You have living relatives, and we know where they are."

I dared not speak for the emotion clenching my throat. I didn't even breathe. I had to hear more.

The Viking smiled magnanimously. When he spoke again, he softened his voice, the sound of gentle menace. "There are many who underestimate my studies"—he cut a look at Alcántara's desk—"but it is only in knowledge that true power lies."

"I have no doubt," I managed. Just as I had no doubt this vampire knew the location and status of every relative and friend valued by each resident on this godforsaken isle.

I had no choice but to do as he asked. I'd retrieve their Acari prize. I'd keep this Annelise Drew alive.

Because if Dagursson knew how to find my family, it meant I could find them, too.

CHAPTER TWO

I'd memorized her file, but nothing could've prepared me for the real Annelise. For the uncertain way she entered the university registrar's building and slipped into line. Her eyes skittered to mine then away again as quickly.

She was raw, an abraded nerve.

No, I told myself, she was just like anyone else. I was just seeking differences, my curiosity sparked by her status as Dagursson's prize. To protect her above all else—I'd never had such an order.

She fidgeted. Chewed on a purple nail. Shoved a preposterous straw fedora low on her head. Insecure or merely impatient?

I sent the full force of my attention to her. My power pulsed outward, beckoning, but still I couldn't catch her eye. A cold sweat broke along my brow, clammy in the overly air-conditioned building.

It was unexpected. Odd. Alarming, almost. Most of these teens were easily snared—especially with my powers. It was a talent I'd mastered long ago, having discovered at a young age that if I concentrated, if I peered deeply into someone's eyes, I could convince anyone of anything. My touch was the most powerful of all; with the proper intent, my hands generated heat that, when directed to another's mind, blanked it of all but my command. It was a rare gift and of particular value to the vampires.

Some called it hypnotism. Others, persuasion. I called it both blessing and curse, because how could trust exist between me and another person when there was such a thing between us? And so, for me, there had never been another person.

Except Charlotte, of course. There'd always been Charlotte. Though, at the time, I'd insisted she didn't count as a real person—she was just my big sister. My pesky Lottie. She'd badgered me, and I'd teased her.

As I remembered Charlotte, a dark craving for revenge burned my throat, wavering my vision. I'd retrieve this girl. I'd do as Dagursson bid. And then I'd find my family.

Concentrating harder, I tried again to enthrall her. Usually my quarry was smoothly baited, reeled in like a fish on a hook. But not Annelise. When she finally snuck another glimpse at me, again she surprised me. While her gaze was arrested, it wasn't by my face—that foolish, meaningless thing that had ensnared so many others. Rather, she was drawn to my arm. To the tattoo marking me: *Le seul paradis c'est le paradis perdu.*

While other recruits were bewitched by this sleepy, wanting expression I assumed—while trying neither to laugh nor despise myself—Annelise was entranced by words, my words. Though not conceived by me, I'd claimed them all the same: *The only paradise is paradise lost.*

I was punished severely when the tattoo was first discovered. Alcántara, with his unrivalled taste for torture, had done the honors. But rather than bearing my punishment in pained silence, I'd fought a perverse desire to smile because my mark was the thing that reminded me my body might've served others, but the innermost part of me, that was yet mine.

The queue in front of the registrar window slowly shrank until it was almost Annelise's turn. For a flicker of a moment I almost felt sorry for her. She thought this would be her first day at university. She'd clawed her way free of her home life, graduating in January with plans to matriculate early to college. But I knew differently. The Directorate had ways of altering plans. A simple thing like university enrollment would pose no challenge. This university would refuse her, and once she left this campus, the next school she knew would be on a rock in the middle of the North Sea.

That or we'd both be dead.

And what if Dagursson's fears proved true? What if she put up a fight? I could always force her to come with me. Other Tracers did.

I dismissed the thought. Even without the Viking's orders to keep her safe, I found the use of force distasteful. It was why I'd so cultivated my talent—thanks to my persuasive powers, my job rarely degraded into coercion.

Would she come willingly? I considered her restless fingers. The way she crushed her hat low over that conspicuously blond hair. There was something in her—a challenge—that spoke of bravery. And yet I saw vulnerability, too, in the downward tilt of her chin.

Afraid, but not fearful.

Unexpected sensations pierced my chest. Sympathy. Curiosity. A hint of fellowship. I wasn't prepared for it.

I hardened my heart.

She was on the Vampire Directorate list. It could've only meant she was as cold and ruthless as any of the other teens who found themselves on the Isle of Night.

It was her turn at the window. I read her expression as she heard the news. The vampires sabotaged her admission, just as they'd orchestrated her acceptance in the first place. Never ones to forsake a cruelly poetic gesture, the Directorate wanted the girl to come to them not merely crushed but destroyed. It was no more or less than the necessary kneading one might give a lump of clay.

But she didn't fall apart at the news, and it surprised me. I'd seen so many others shriek and curse their fates—boys and girls alike—but not this Annelise. Instead, I watched as a strange transformation occurred. Somehow she stood taller, seemed older. I realized it was pride I was witnessing. Self-worth. Courage. Dignity.

I'd thought I knew this candidate, but I obviously hadn't understood her depths, not truly. On the flight over, I'd prepared as I always did—reviewing photos, observing surveillance-camera footage, poring through medical records. This morning, I'd squinted at Annelise through binocular lenses. I knew her standardized test scores, middle school grade point average, and iPod playlist. Despite her petite stature and long, white-blond hair, it was clear she'd fashioned herself an outsider. Beyond this, however, I had no clue.

She stepped out of line, and I faded into the shadows. The next time she saw me would be in the parking lot, where I'd already disabled the engine of her Honda.

I'd budgeted sixty minutes to get her into my car. Sixty more to reach the airstrip by the appointed time. Two hours total in which to convince her.

I had my orders. There was no choice; she must come with me. I rolled my shoulders, already tasting the self-loathing that was the price of my persuasive talents.

Standing in the blazing sun of the car lot, I watched from afar, waiting while she struggled to turn the ignition. She scraped tears from her eyes, and the abrupt jerk of her wrist had me wondering if she was more angry than sad. I had to perceive the difference if I was to convince her. To charm her.

But still I waited. I gave it a good long time, too,

knowing it'd surely reached over thirty-eight degrees Celsius in her rust bucket by now. She'd be ready for me.

I had this in the bag.

Finally, I approached. Leaning against the driver's-side window, I peered down at her. She struck me as so small in the seat of that ancient car, but I forced away the thought, sending a blast of my power down instead, beckoning her, drawing her to me.

I flexed my outstretched arm, and though I'd cursed the Florida heat, it served me well now, dampening my shirt, making it cling in a way that'd served me well in the past. I gave her my most charming smile. "Trouble?"

But when her eyes flicked to me, they only skittered away again. And there it was, another deviation from the norm. It was in the set of her jaw, a fierce determination to overcome this obstacle as she'd stood up to so many others. She didn't want my help. Didn't want to need it.

Annelise had self-respect, and she clung to it. Clung to her goals. She wouldn't be distracted by any pretty boy, no matter how intently I flexed.

"Lift the bonnet for me, aye?" I told her, but then I cursed myself the moment it was out of my mouth. I'd intended to express concern, but my words had come too softly. I had to be careful—the line between feigning sympathy and actually feeling it was a fine one.

She complied, finally, and opened the hood. But as I leaned over and studied the engine, I felt her studying me. Never had someone's attention felt so heavy on my skin.

I fought to shake the feeling, making myself concentrate, instead, on my surroundings. This place was so repellent, so alien. The sun was relentless, beating at us from all around. The heat, claustrophobic and inescapable. And the smells…car exhaust, hot tarmac underfoot, and hanging over it all, a sultry Florida stench, thick and cloying like tropical fruit left to rot in the heat. *Eyja næturinnar* might've been a hostile, detestable place, but the air was clean, and when I surfed, the waves pummeled me in a way that felt as though they might purify my soul.

I realized I'd been frozen in place, leaning against the bloody hood. I knew damn well what was wrong with her car—I was the one who'd messed with the carburetor in the first place. But I just stood there, knowing her eyes were on me. Was I inviting her perusal? Was I that proud and idiotic?

Time to focus. For bloody real.

I stood, and sure enough, I spotted her blush, saw how her gaze pulled away but didn't know where to land. She had been eyeing me.

I was in control again. Clapping the grease from my hands, I told her, "I think it's your carb."

Her smile was tentative, as if she was just practicing. "The only carb I know is the bagel I had for breakfast."

It took me a moment to realize she'd made a joke. I'd been too distracted by the sound of her voice. Quiet, but husky, too. The richness of it was a startling contrast to her tiny figure.

A tight laugh escaped her. She held herself stiffly, as though she'd forgotten how to stand. I'd let the silence hang too long, and she'd mistaken my stare for something else. Criticism, maybe. I imagined she was well acquainted with the feeling.

"Kidding," she said. "I know you meant carburetor. Internal combustion…" And then she muttered something more that I didn't catch.

She looked stricken, uneasy in her own skin. She was so brittle. Achingly vulnerable. And so obviously lonely.

She wasn't the sort of girl people would've sought out. For the first time, I saw what Dagursson had meant about the similarities between this girl and my sister. Both were too smart, too sensitive, too strange.

But unlike Charlotte, Annelise's differences made her

self-conscious. Like a creature incapable of camouflage, this girl would've remained an alien among her peers.

The other recruits on the Isle—female and male alike—would scent her weakness, and like a pack of jackals, they'd attack. She wouldn't survive the week.

But I could protect her, I realized—just as Dagursson ordered.

I felt a shimmer of longing. I *would* protect her. I'd help her as I'd been unable to help my sister. Hope blurred my vision, so vividly it was like a physical thing in the air around me, flaring brighter and even more painful than the Florida sun.

I blinked it away. *No.* I needed distance and focus.

I'd protect her because it was my job. Because it was the only way I'd find my family.

I tuned out then. I pushed this person, Annelise, to the edge of my mind until she was just a shadow on my periphery, and only then did I go through the motions, exercising the mechanics of my charisma.

When she accepted a ride, I knew I had her.

Like all the other recruits, Annelise wouldn't be missed. Nobody would notice she was gone, or if they did, they wouldn't care.

Still more thoughts to be quickly shoved away.

I'd gotten her into my car, and now I needed to get her onto the plane. As we cruised down the road, I amped up the charm. I reached for it, second nature by now, and power buzzed along my skin, vibrating toward her in the tiny cockpit of my sports car.

But my control shattered. The car swerved. I quickly recovered.

My own goddamned power had bounced back and slapped me.

I scrubbed a hand over my face. *Bloody hell.* Echoes of it rippled along my skin, making the hair on my arms stand on end.

She drew in a sharp breath, then whispered, "Oh God."

She'd felt it, too.

Who was this girl? I needed to wrest control of this exchange before I turned off the road and drove us somewhere private so I could find out.

I needed to appeal to intellect, not emotion. I steeled my voice. "*God*, is it? Do you believe in God, Annelise?"

"*Somebody* had enough irony to pack 185 IQ points into a blond head," she said without waiting a beat.

I shocked both of us when I laughed. Hard.

Such ease—it was foreign to me. Pleasant. But mostly it was dangerous.

I told myself this flirtation felt comfortable and good simply because I was talented at my job. It certainly wasn't because I was enjoying myself.

By the time we reached the airstrip, I'd sufficiently gathered myself. I was back on my guard and acutely attuned to the doubt and disbelief on her face as she studied the small jet. She knew better than most young women how things that seemed too good to be true rarely were.

I was losing her.

This had never happened to me before—not at this stage in the game. There were two recruits waiting on the plane, and by the time they'd reached this point, they were practically clawing at each other to see who could board first.

I made it a rule never to touch the girls, but I had no choice now.

I extended my power, reaching out for her shoulder. My power had backfired before—what would happen now when I actually touched her?

Tentative, I let my hand alight on her shoulder. I felt the warmth of her body through her shirt—a vintage Pretenders concert tee—and memories swamped me in a flood so overpowering I almost broke the connection. Flashes of secret, stolen moments, of early missions that'd taken me to underground clubs, of brief sweet tastes of rebellion and freedom. Of a youth stolen from me.

Slowly, slowly, I slid my hand higher, wanting to feel her skin under my fingertips just once. Finally, I reached the nape of her neck. Hair so soft and fine brushed the back of my hand, sending a jolt up my arm.

It took supreme concentration to keep a hold on my power and not do something foolish. To remind myself I was a Tracer and not some normal guy parked in a car with a normal girl.

Power was vibrating back at me full force. My throat sounded rusty as I asked her, "Are you ready to embrace a whole new life?"

A part of me no longer knew what it was I referred to.

She shifted away from me, breaking the spell.

"Why me?" she asked, and the uncertainty was back, thick in her voice. Somehow my control had slipped again.

I shifted, too, closer to her. I was too near to my goal to lose her now. Dagursson would kill me for my failure. But, mostly, I found I was curious to see what she'd do next. How she'd act on the plane, with the other students, in her studies. How life on the Isle of Night would be with her on it.

"Why not you, Annelise?" I asked.

I was intrigued. Humbled. Because maybe Dagursson was right. Maybe this young woman was stronger than any of us imagined.

Did she have the potential to become even be more powerful than the vampires themselves? It was something to consider.

But then she flinched away, breaking contact. It was enough to remind me. She was just a child. A job to be done.

I eased back in my seat, surreptitiously checking my watch. I had ten minutes to get her on that plane before people started asking questions.

I forced myself back into autopilot.

Pretending incredulity, I asked, "Are you saying you don't want to leave Florida? The Gulfstream IV can travel over 4,000 nautical miles." In my experience, technical gibberish impressed vulnerable minds.

But Annelise's mind was far from vulnerable. Her reply was quick. "Oh, well, that's a relief," she said. "Particularly as I generally calculate things in terms of nautical miles."

This time, I had to bite my cheek not to laugh. All the better that my resulting expression was a silent glare.

She inhaled deeply, seeming to gather her thoughts.

I found I was curious to hear them.

"I mean, yes," she said at last. "Of course. I *long* to leave Florida." Her voice was so low I had to strain to hear. For the first time, she was being upfront with me rather than using humor as a shield. My reaction was mingled fear that she'd speak too intimately and pleasure that she might. "My life here…it's been hard. I've always dreamt of leaving."

Once again, her eyes darted from mine. She was vulnerable. An open wound.

What was I doing to this girl? She should've been somewhere else. Anywhere else. She deserved to be with people who loved her.

But such notions were dangerous.

The university parking lot seemed miles away now. There, I'd expected she'd eventually annoy me. Now I just wanted to hear what she'd say next.

I reached for her, touched her chin. Whatever I was doing, I couldn't stop.

The bones of her face were so delicate, her cheeks dewy with the lingering dampness of sweat, or tears. Her jaw pulsed under my fingers, clenching and releasing, the movement as fragile and determined as a bird's beating wings. She was so troubled.

I found I wanted to ease her mind. I turned her to face

me. "I'll take you someplace very far away," I heard myself say, my voice a rasp in my throat. I told myself these intimate words were all a function of my master plan—nothing more. But a part of me allowed myself to pretend I meant more. "Far from your father. From the people who don't understand you."

In that moment, I believed what I was saying, even as I recognized the lies within. Because in that moment, I believed I knew her. Believed I understood.

There was such raw trust on her face as she asked, "Where are we going?"

I pulled away then, gripped the steering wheel. She'd believed my every word. I was about to sucker yet another child onto the Isle of Night. And now she'd asked where I was taking her. How could I lie?

Somehow I felt I owed her some bit of sincerity. I had to find a half-truth that wouldn't send her screaming from the car. "Far away," I finally said. "Life as you know it will change utterly."

And so it was truth enough. I saw the light change in her eyes as she accepted my words, made her decision.

She trusted me. She'd get on the plane with me. And I'd take her to a place of savage cruelty. To her almost-certain death.

My family, I reminded myself. I was doing this to find my family.

This was just a girl. She was nobody to me. She could never be anybody to me.

In fact, prized as she was by the Directorate, she might only pose a danger to me. I'd believed she was different from the other kids, the gangbangers and juvie rejects, but maybe it was more than potential strength that set Annelise apart. Maybe her game was deeper and more sinister than I could fathom. For all I knew, she was playing me right now.

"Far away?" she repeated. "Are we going west?"

It seemed a childish thing to ask. Was the naïveté an act? Rarely did I feel this sort of uncertainty, and it shortened my temper. "No," I said. "We're leaving the country. For an island."

She looked intrigued, as if I'd packed her a weekend bag and was sweeping her away to Hawaii for a quick getaway.

"Not that kind of island," I said in a voice colder than I'd intended. "It's far away," I added, softening my tone. She wasn't on the plane yet; I could still lose her. "Far north. North of Scotland. North of the Shetlands. It's a dark place. A cold place."

She shifted in her seat, hand poised on the door latch. She'd decided. The bait was taken. The open trust on her face floored me.

She wasn't the one gaming me; it was I who'd betrayed her. Annelise was no schemer. She was just a girl who wanted to escape her pain. Little did she know, I was taking her to a place that'd invented the meaning of the word.

Part of me wished she'd back out. I had the strange sense that, in winning her consent, I'd somehow lost something else. I was just unable to put my finger on what.

"So what's this island called?" she asked, and the lightness in her tone leached oxygen from the small space. Suddenly it was unbearably hot in that ridiculous sports car.

"Those who speak the old tongue call it *Eyja næturinnar,*" I told her. "The Isle of Night."

The island had two names, as so many things in my world. Fitting, seeing as she used two names as well. She went by Drew, but I refused to call her this. It was the name of the man whose home she'd once lived in, not her own.

From that day on, to me, she would always be Annelise.

CHAPTER THREE

Present day

"Stubborn, human boy," Freya flings the words at me as though a foul taste needs to be spewed from her body. "You will not return to the Isle of Night. I forbid it." The resonant hum of her voice ripples across my skin, filling the small cave. She is Vampire. The mere sound of her voice can stop a man's heart in his chest.

"Listen to the lady," Carden tells me. He's gripping my arm, holding me back. He's Vampire, too, and it makes him stronger than me—a fact I pretend not to hate. He'd been young, brawny, and well made as a human, which means he's all the fiercer as one of the undead.

I stare down at his hand. I'd come merely to give my report, and now it seems they're not going to let me leave. "Is this the only reason you're here, McCloud? You're an enforcer now?" Technically, Carden and I are allies, both serving Freya as double agents in the takedown of the Directorate. It doesn't mean I trust him.

He laughs. "Someone's got to mind the riffraff. Come, lad, why do you want to go back to a crap place like *Eyja næturinnar* anyway?"

Freya ignores Carden's casual comments, but the half-circle of figures surrounding her—female vampires of varying ages—make their distaste clear.

"I've got a job to do," I say simply.

Protect Annelise. It's the drumbeat of my heart. *Annelise.*

She's in everyone's sights now. All semester, she fielded attacks from bloodthirsty Trainees. Eager for answers, she's even become Alcántara's assistant to spy on him. She's closing in on the truth and needs an ally more than ever. More, she needs a friend. Carden comes and goes. He keeps his own schedule and has his own motivations, which means he's not always around to watch her back.

"Your job there is done, Ronan." Freya's voice intensifies, an unearthly sound that prickles gooseflesh up my spine. "I need you here. Or have you forgotten? Here is where we wage war against the Directorate. *Eilean Ban-Laoch* is where you belong."

Eilean Ban-Laoch, the island of warrior women. It's also my secret home base. Here, the female vampires rule—older even than the Norsemen on the Isle of Night, they keep the ways of the ancient Celts, seeking a return to the old order. And Freya is the most ancient and unyielding of all.

"So I'm a prisoner in my own home?" I force a half-smile to downplay the tension in the small cavern. "I wouldn't have returned if I'd known I wouldn't be allowed to leave again."

Freya's pale eyes bore into me, her features gone utterly still. I've misstepped—it seems I don't do casual as effortlessly as Carden.

"You're no prisoner," she says. "Unless you wish to be?" Power is vibrating from her now. It's a tangible, foreign thing, like electricity, both alluring and repellent.

"No, indeed." I give her a respectful half-bow. I'm used to dealing with male vampires—the same vampires who'd have everyone believe that men are the only ones capable of immortality—but it's women who are the world's creators, its givers of life, and so female vampires are the strongest of all. "It's only that there's one more thing I must do on the Isle of Night," I explain. The sheer force of my will is what enables me to hold her gaze.

"A *thing* you must do." She gives Carden a wicked look. "Perhaps he's referring to a certain Acari named Annelise Drew?"

Carden jostles my arm. He laughs, and it has the ring of triumph to it. When it comes to Annelise, we are playing a game he thinks he's won. I ignore him.

"It's no secret I want to protect her," I say.

At first, I watched over Annelise because Freya ordered it. That the Directorate also wanted her alive suggests she holds the mysterious key to their destruction. But one day I realized: Now I protect her because I want to.

Freya snaps, "Carden has sole charge of the girl's well-being."

"I'm taking care of our wee dove just fine," he says. When I try to jerk my arm free, he sees something on my face—the tremendous desire to punch him perhaps—and he winks.

Freya's sharp voice cuts between us. "Enough. Ronan, your role on *Eyja næturinnar* is over."

Even though I feel her impatience pulsing over me, I bow my head lower to try again. I can't abandon Annelise now. "I am merely eager to continue to act as your agent, keeping an eye on things in the field."

Freya considers me. "You mean, 'keep an eye on the girl.'" She clearly thinks my feelings begin and end on a part of my anatomy located somewhat south of my heart. "I believe this Annelise is your weakness."

She's wrong. Annelise is my strength.

But let Freya think what she will—I won't sway. "I'm

deeply entrenched in Alcántara's world," I explain, keeping to my original line of reason. "As his Tracer, I'm more well suited than anyone to remain an active agent."

Carden's low laugh bounces off the walls of the crude cavern, grating my nerves. "More well suited, is it? Unless you're talking about that getup you wear to splash about in the waves, I can't say I agree." I jerk away from him, but he only grins, his hand wrapped around my arm like a manacle. "Fret not, pup. I've got things covered on the Isle."

Things… He means Annelise.

"I've taken her as a mate," he adds with a smile.

"By accident." My retort is instant, my hostility foolish, but I can't help myself. When she'd come back from that first mission *bonded* to Carden… My rage boils at the memory. I'd sensed my feelings for her before then, but the moment I knew I couldn't have her? That was when I realized I couldn't live without her. "She was the one who bonded the both of you," I manage. "Unintentionally, as I recall."

Such disrespect against any vampire other than the easygoing Carden would've meant my immediate death, but the Scotsman only grins and gives a playful slug to my arm. "I think our young Ronan is just sore I've got the better job." The murder in my eyes grows as he broadens his smile. "I think the whelp would like to hit me." He slings a rough arm around my shoulder then, speaking to me in a consoling tone that makes my jaw clench. "Don't get yourself into a lather. You know I've a true affection for the chit."

I give a sharp tug to my arm, breaking free at last from his grip. "What is this, the eighteenth century? Annelise isn't a…what'd you call her…a *chit*?"

Finally, I see Carden's eyes go cold. "Easy, boy," he says, seizing my shoulder. "You'd do well to mind your affections. Aye, she's no chit. Trust me, I know better than any how Annelise is a woman."

His words tighten around my chest like a vise. I say

through clenched teeth, "She thinks you love her."

"And love her I do." The coldness in Carden's eyes has been replaced by something unreadable. "But I won't let my feelings about her cloud our most important goal. We must triumph over the Directorate. Whatever the cost. Drew would be the first to agree."

"You think? I'd have guessed you'd list her safety as the primary goal."

"It's called honor, boy. We learned it in forty-five."

"The year 1745 was a long time ago, McCloud. Your Scottish honor has nothing to do with vampires." I give him a peremptory smile. "We're friends with the Brits now, you know."

"I'll tell you what I do know," he says, and I can see the smirk in his eyes already, damn him. "I reckon you've got a puppy crush on a lass, and it's got your knickers in a bunch. You young bucks are all the same."

That's where he's wrong. I was raised in isolation, weaned on savagery. My body might be nineteen, but my soul is old as the cave we stand in. In my heart, I'm as ancient as any vampire.

"Older doesn't always mean wiser," I say, and before Carden can respond, I turn to Freya. I choke down my anger, forcing myself to remember why I've allied with one set of vampires to take down another. Carden might be a son of a bitch and Freya power hungry, but Alcántara's Directorate is an evil I could never destroy on my own. "I'm young, it's true. But I've served you well."

"Don't speak to me of *serving*," she snaps. "The time has come for you to *obey*."

I don't flinch because I know I obey nothing but my own heart. And my heart tells me nobody can protect Annelise like I will.

Freya's eyes harden on me. "Perhaps you need a lesson. Shall I tell you of Sonja?" I recognize the name instantly, from the runes Annelise found carved into a cliffside. I don't know much about the inner workings of the Directorate, but one more piece has fallen into place. "Must I tell you how Sonja, my…*sister*," she spits, "my spoiled little sister, turned on us? She's like a child playing at queen, and when she didn't get her way, she took everything—our secrets, our treasures, our lore—and used it against us. Must I remind you how her perverse army of…of *boys* has nearly decimated us? It's taken us centuries to rebuild the female vampire population. We can't just run about biting girls, you know. Few survive the transformation. Those of the purest blood have the hardest time of all."

I want to ask, what of the males? Sons are rare. We Tracers are few, all of us kept in ignorance. Are we also of this line? Am I? But I dare not ask such provocative questions—Freya has slaughtered people more valuable than me for less.

Carden grins and gives my arm a shake, as though he's in a pub instead of this miserable, airless cave. "Buck up, lad. You're just jealous that while you were off babysitting the others, I was bonding to our wee Annelise."

I look away, unable to meet his eyes, lest he see the truth of his words there. "I helped Annelise long before you were in the picture."

"But I'm in the picture now, aren't I?" Carden tsks in that patronizing way of his, shaking his head at me. "Poor Ronan. Seems like you got the short end of the stick. I keep Drew *close*"—he emphasizes the word—"and you've only—"

I cut him off, defending myself to Freya. "Against all odds, I've helped keep Acari Drew alive for you."

And yet, in my most secret of hearts is a different truth.

I've kept her alive for me.

"As it should be," Freya says. She reaches up and strokes the hand of one of her lackeys. "All my girls are of the highest lineage. Annelise, too." Her tolerant, instructive tone makes her sound like a dog trainer. "We are all family."

I avert my eyes. This creepy "family" is the last thing Annelise would want.

"One by one," Freya continues, "I will save the children of my children. I will make them stronger. Mine will be the most powerful coven the world has ever known."

I struggle to make sense of her intentions. Annelise would rather die than become Vampire.

Or maybe I'm wrong. Maybe Annelise would want this life.

Loss—the potential of it—clouds my vision for a moment. Need stabs me. I've already lost so much. I will lose no more.

I remember all we've shared. I think back to the Directorate Challenge. It'd been at the end of her first term here, when she'd faced her nemesis and almost died. Such trials require mental strength as much as physical. I believe in my heart it was partly my support that pulled her through.

I cut my eyes to Carden. The connection I share with Annelise protects her more than any vampire guard dog could. The bond we share is stronger than any chemical reaction.

And yet he claims to love her.

Maybe I don't know either of them at all. Carden is easy and charming in a way that makes girls want him—in a way I've never managed, at least not without relying on my powers. Maybe Annelise's heart's desire is to become Vampire and live forever by his side. Maybe.

Or maybe not. It's a hope that keeps me going.

If I don't know Annelise's heart yet, there's still time to learn.

"I'll continue your fight in secret," I say. I'm past nerves, past defiance. All I know is I need to get back. "You have every reason to keep me installed on *Eyja næturinnar.*"

"No," Freya says crisply. "I need you here. We muster our forces here. *All* our forces. Sonja's massacre of ancients decimated us, but our strength is rebuilding."

"Please, Mistress Freya."

She leans forward from the shadows. With her tilted head and narrowed eyes, she considers me as one might a plate of food. I don't often resort to pleading, and she knows it. She also knows leverage when she sees it.

Suddenly, she sits back with a sharp sniff. "As you wish, Ronan. There is one way I'll let you leave."

"Name it," I say too quickly. Her concession is more than I expected. I have no choice but to comply with her wishes, whatever they may be. Like any good sergeant taking orders from his general, I bow my head and brace for it. "What is my assignment?"

"If you truly wish to return, then it won't trouble you to kill Alrik Dagursson."

I peer up, caught off guard. "I beg your pardon?"

"Master Alrik Dagursson," she says. Her patronizing tone makes it clear I'm trying her patience. "*He* is your assignment. Or will you refuse this request, too?"

My reaction is instant. *Can't. Won't.*

"It's decided," she says calmly. "Promise me you'll kill Dagursson, and I will allow you to return to that place. To that beloved"—she waves a dismissive hand—"*rock* of yours."

"But—"

"There…is…no…*but*." Her power fills the cave, surrounding me, like a force pressing on me. It feels as though the air has been sucked from the cave, making my blood roar and my skin buzz. "Unless your plan is to kill Alrik, you are forbidden to leave this island."

I'm not even certain I understand. I've never been asked to assassinate a vampire—and Dagursson isn't just any vampire. He's one of the Directorate's inner circle. He's ancient. A Viking. Impossibly powerful. Likely invincible. To try to murder him would mean my death.

"You wish me to…kill him?" I repeat, buying time to think. Dying isn't what bothers me—I know firsthand that there are worse things a man can endure. I refuse to kill Dagursson until I discover what he knows of my family.

"Yes. Kill, Ronan. You remember how to kill. You will dispatch Alrik Dagursson in whichever way you see fit. Slay him. Stake him." She gives a bored wave of her hand. "Immolation, decapitation, exsanguination…however you wish to do it." Her eyes meet and hold mine for a long moment. "Does this trouble you?"

I dare not tell her the truth—I won't share my vulnerability with any vampire. "It's too great a risk," is the excuse I use instead. "Dagursson is powerful. If I attempt an assassination and fail, I risk exposing everything we've worked for. Perhaps if I were to kill Alcántara instead—"

She waves that away. "Yes, yes, I know your thoughts on Hugo. You suspect he killed your family, et cetera, et cetera. And I tell you Alcántara is just a pawn. A dog, panting for scraps. But Dagursson…" She gives a wolfish smile. "He is the keeper of their lore. He knows much about our history, our lineage. And knowledge is their primary weapon against us—take that away and they have nothing."

I picture him in Alcántara's office, bent over an ancient scroll. Knowledge makes him impossibly powerful. He is the keeper of Freya's bloodline. My own.

The need to know what he knows warps my vision. "Usually I unquestioningly execute your orders, and yet—"

"Then *execute* Alrik," she says at once. Power fills the cave even more thickly and robs the air from my lungs. "I have had enough of your impertinence, child." Though she speaks in barely a whisper, her voice echoes painfully in my skull. "You will kill Alrik Dagursson, or I will kill your Annelise."

An invisible force seizes my throat—clutching, squeezing, choking. It's fear. I forgot what it felt like. "I beg your pardon?"

Candlelight catches her yellow hair and gleams. Her smile, too, gleams. She's amused now, like a bullying schoolgirl—but her fangs, long and shining, remind me she hasn't been a girl for over a thousand years.

Rather than answer me, she turns to address the female vampires standing at silent attention behind her. "Do you see, my daughters? Do you see how this is perhaps a good idea regardless? If Annelise were dead, then our Ronan wouldn't want to return to his precious Isle of Night. Annelise would make a worthy vampire, it's true"—she pauses thoughtfully—"and yet she'd be just as worthy a sacrifice. She strikes me as overly headstrong anyhow. Such a tedious trait in a young woman." She pauses and nods with exaggerated consideration. "And to think she's become close with Alcántara."

"They're not close," I dare cut in.

She freezes. "So sure, are you?" Her eyes linger on me for a protracted moment. Finally, she shrugs. "It's a concern nonetheless. If something happens to make me doubt her, if Annelise finds herself on the wrong side of things and becomes Alcántara's creature…" She shakes her head in mock remorse. "I'd rather see her dead than watch her fall under the influence of the Directorate."

I cut my eyes to Carden. Why isn't he speaking up? But I see no outrage on his face. Does he believe this too? "What say you, McCloud?" I spit his clan name at him. "Are you so blinded by loyalty to your quest that you'd see Annelise as collateral damage?"

"*Our* quest, lad. Our quest is greater than any one person. It will outlive all of us. Annelise included."

"Is that what your bloody Scottish honor tells you?"

"Ronan." Freya gives a stern clap to her hands. "This is

not a game. Annelise's potential is too great—if Alcántara channels it, he'll become too powerful. She is my flesh and blood—her fate is my decision. And I have decided you will kill Alrik. Or you'll pay with Annelise's life."

Dagursson. He's the only one who knows how to find my family. The thought consumes me.

I bow my head. Swallow my pain. There is no choice. Annelise needs my protection more than ever. "Consider it done."

CHAPTER FOUR

I squint my eyes, trying to focus on my watch's glowing LED numbers without breaking my stride. I thought a hard run before class would purge the noise from my head, but instead, each pounding step of my feet is a gunshot blast spiraling thoughts through my brain.

What haven't I taught Annelise?

What will she need?

What doesn't she know?

What will keep her alive?

What if I fail to kill Dagursson? What if I'm killed, and Freya comes gunning for her? What if Carden is too preoccupied with his quest to protect Annelise at a critical moment? What if she is alone and needs to escape?

And there is my answer: Navigation. That's what I'll teach today.

I check my watch. *Bloody hell.* My pace has been too brutal—I'm way ahead of schedule. All the snow has melted, leaving mucky gravel in its place, and I skid my feet along the path to slow.

If I arrive too soon, Annelise will approach me. She'll try to talk.

Her talk unmans me.

I have to keep my focus. It's too easy to lose myself to dreadful what-ifs. What if Freya had prevented my return, and Annelise had thought I'd simply dropped off the face of the earth? Carden wouldn't exactly have raced to tell her the truth about me—of that I have no doubt.

I stop completely, bend and stretch and catch my breath. My shirt is nearly soaked through, but no amount of sweat can steal the chill from my bones.

I check my watch again. Class in three. I make the slow walk down the hillside to the beach where I teach a Primitive Skills Intensive to Initiates, the few second-year Acari who remain.

Annelise is down by the shore, squatting and picking at shells. I always feel a shot of relief at the sight of her. *She is here. Alive. Safe.*

Her head pops up instantly, eyes going straight to me. A smile blooms on her face.

Good Christ, seeing *me* has done this to her.

Like the sun through parting clouds, a wave of heat rolls through me, melting the knot of ice that's been lodged in my gut since I stood in Freya's cave. Annelise and I are here together. We are in this thing, together.

The effort it takes to hide my pleasure is tremendous. Almost impossible. I grit my teeth and focus on the burning in my lungs instead. There's the ghost of a stitch in my side. I embrace it.

I jerk my attention to the others. Only half a dozen Initiates are left in my class, and I watch them along the rocky shoreline as they poke at some poor creature washed ashore. "It's time," I call. Measuring my tone has made it overly harsh. I don't care. On this island, shows of kindness are deadly. "Class. Now."

As the Initiates stand and stalk up the beach toward me, the difference between them and their fallen classmates is clear. Lithe and catsuited, they have the grace of predators. They are savagery and hunger, weapons in female form. They are a sight to behold—and their attention is zeroed in on me.

There are men who'd envy my position. Those men are fools.

This time next year, there will be even fewer survivors from this class. While a small fraction of male students successfully transition from Trainees to Vampire, even fewer of the females endure the ascension from Acari to Initiate to Guidon to finally become the cream of the cream, the most elite, a Watcher.

Annelise could make it, I think, and as I do, I feel her appear by my side. "You're back," she says under her breath as we wait for the rest of the girls.

"Aye," I manage. I want to turn, to stand closer, but force myself to ignore her.

I feel her smirk as she says, "You're doing the secretive thing again."

"Aye," I repeat blandly, knowing it'll coax a laugh from her. It's unwise, like a stupid, sodding schoolboy, but her laugh warms me even more than her smile.

"Okay, be that way." She pauses. "I worried you left me," she says, her tone uneasy. Earlier this term, Carden left her for weeks. She must've thought it was my turn.

I let myself look at her, finally. "I'm here," I say, infusing my voice with a gravity I hope she hears. "I'm not leaving."

Something eases around her eyes, setting them alight, and I have to look away.

"Good," she says, perky once more. "They had Otto subbing this Wilderness Workshop of yours"—she shoots me a challenging grin, unable to resist teasing the name of my class—"and it just wasn't the same. He's way too metrosexual to be teaching us how to, like, find and treat water. He strikes me as more a how-to-find-and-treat-your-espresso-while-in-Berlin kinda guy."

I shoot her a scolding look. I didn't time this right at all. I should've slowed my pace sooner than I did. This is way too much time alone with her. Way too much biting my cheek not to smile.

She sidles closer. "I need to talk to you."

I stiffen. She's too close. Her hair carries a sweet, clean scent, like pears, and it startles me.

I shift away, but we've moved at the same time, and her arm brushes mine. The warmth of her, so near to me, prickles my skin with goose bumps. My muscles seize, my back stiffening. I cup a hand around my mouth to yell down the beach. "Party's over, ladies. Double time it. Let's get to work."

"Seriously, Ronan." She sounds so urgent, so alone and needy.

I can't resist it, can't resist her.

"I heard you," I say quietly. "Later. We'll talk in the dining hall."

"No, it needs to be private." She edges closer. "Can we walk back together?"

Together. How that would be…

I edge away. "That's no good." Too many eyes are watching us.

"Tonight?"

"There's something I need to do tonight." Stake out Dagursson. Maybe even *stake* Dagursson. I need to get this mission over with. I need to focus. Survive. Make sure I can stay here. Near her.

"Then when, Ronan?" The others are getting closer, and she's spoken to me in a whisper, her husky voice a quiet murmur at my side. "There's something I have to tell you."

Ten thousand scenarios shoot through my head, each one a fiery comet of possibility.

"Tomorrow." My voice has grown cold, but I don't know

any other way. I don't know how to do this. "Catch me after breakfast tomorrow."

She shrugs. I feel how tense she is, how anxious and preoccupied, but I can't let it get to me. Can't let *her* get to me, not when I have this suicide mission ahead of me.

I dive into my lecture.

"Orienteering," I say loudly. "Who knows what it is?" Annelise begins to speak, and I cut her off. "Someone else. Isabella?" I turn to the auburn-haired Initiate who's been on my blacklist since she and her friend tried to drown Annelise in the surf.

The girl gapes at me with a look of profound boredom. "Isn't that what you do, like, on the first day of something?"

"You can't be serious," Annelise mutters.

"You're thinking of the word *orientation*," I say quickly, before the two have a chance to get into it. "Technically, orienteering is a sport, though it began as a military exercise. Think of it as navigation. How to find your way through rough countryside quickly."

I spent months turning Annelise into a strong swimmer. I taught her how to use a grappling hook, how to land a fall. I drilled her through one-armed push-ups, wind sprints, and endless kip-ups. And now, if she ever needs to make a quick escape off the island, I want to make sure she'll know how to find her way.

"Can't the vamps just give us a GPS like the rest of civilization?" someone asks.

"No GPS," I say with exaggerated patience. "And what's more, for our purposes, you won't have a map or compass either."

Annelise gives Isabella a broad smile. "Seeing as you have no moral compass, that shouldn't be a stretch."

"Acari Drew," I snap. My affection for her runs deep, but in class I have to treat her as I would any other student…even if the joke was a good one. "I appreciate your wordplay, but please let me do the lecturing."

She tips her head, hiding a grin. "Yes, Tracer Ronan."

Isabella's eyes narrow on us. The red-haired Acari isn't exactly the vampires' pet, but I have seen her chatty with one of Headmaster Fournier's staff. It'd be the death of me and Annelise both if we presented anything other than the picture of propriety…and I fear we're not succeeding.

I turn from Annelise. I need to get my head in the game. If I'm going to assassinate a member of the Directorate and live to see the next day, I need total focus.

Which means I need Annelise someplace where she can't give me her smile.

A solution hits me. I tell the girls, "Tonight you'll be driven to the far end of the island. You'll navigate your way home using the stars."

I feel Annelise's reaction the instant the words are out of my mouth. *Bloody hell.* I catch her eye, sending her a flash of sympathy so brief only she'd notice. The assignment would rake up painful memories for her, being so similar to a punishment she'd endured when she'd first arrived on the island. It'd been the thing that bonded her to Emma, her best friend…Emma, whose death she blames on herself.

Our eyes meet, and she gives me the hint of a nod. She's okay, and of course she is. She's got a spine of steel. She is resolved. She's a survivor. She's my Ann.

I continue my lecture on autopilot. It's one I've given before. And the discussion goes much as it has before. The same questions—some thoughtful, some inane. I can tell by a student's question whether or not she'll make it. Whether she'll survive in a fundamental way. It takes more than savagery to be a skilled Watcher. A Watcher is clever and smart, cool under pressure. She can assemble a homemade weapon as easily as making an omelet. She knows what to say and how to say it—in a variety of languages.

"Take a heading," I tell them.

"What's a heading?"

"Find a distant spot in the landscape—a certain rock, there are all kinds of options on this island—and head toward it."

"Why do you need a heading?"

"You might wander in circles without one."

"How do you know what direction you're going?"

"Look at the sun to orient yourself." I find the sun in the sky and point to it. "The sun rises in the east and sets in the west. People have used sundials for centuries. They work. Put a stake in the ground, and watch as the shadow falls in different spots as the sun moves through the sky. Actually, that's your assignment for the afternoon. Make a sundial. See if you can tell me what time it is."

There's a round of moaning. One of them whines, "That sounds hard."

I raise a brow. "Survival is hard, Acari."

"I thought our assignment was to find our way across the island," another says.

"That's tonight."

"How will we find our way without the sun?"

"Simple," I tell them. "Find the North Star. It never moves."

"Establish true north," Annelise adds. She rolls her eyes, her way to say *duh*.

It was a meaningless aside, but for a moment, I'm gutted. *True north.* It's what Annelise has become to me. I hadn't known hope before I met her, not really. When I'm with her, I feel renewed. I have possibilities. I feel known.

"How do you find the North Star?" someone asks.

I can't find my voice, but Ann answers for me, and it's a mercy. "It's at the very tip of the handle of the Little Dipper." She's dropped to her knees, already at work sketching out the face of her sundial. "It's the bright one," she adds dismissively, concentrating on drawing lines in the sand.

"You can't miss it."

"Can't you just find that, then?" another student asks.

My eyes keep returning to Annelise, mesmerized by her focused intent. She's proud—she'll want to be the first one to finish this assignment.

"Tracer Ronan?"

I shake the nonsense from my head. "You can't always have your true north." There's a pathetic metaphor in there somewhere.

"Why not?"

I shrug, growing impatient, eyes once more landing on Annelise. She's digging in the side of her boot to pull out a throwing star. She'll use that instead of a stick to cast a shadow for her sundial. "Because something might get in the way," I say distractedly. She's so clever, working through the assignment—it's like I can see the cogs spinning in her head. "Like a body of water, or…" I must focus on class but can't look away. She's planting the star in the sand. There's a flash of blue-white glare as light catches the steel. "Or some other natural element, like a—" I spot a design etched along its face—the pattern of a bird's wing. It's the star Carden gave her. Jealousy stabs me.

"Like a…?" a female voice prompts.

Annelise tilts her face to me, giving me an inquisitive look.

"Or a"—I rack my brain, trying to remember what I was saying, remember how to breathe—"Like anything. You might walk into a crevasse. A lake. A monster. Enough talking," I finish sharply. "Get to work."

Carden's gift to Annelise is a reminder: I have to stop gaping at her. There is only one thing I can afford to see, and that's Dagursson, and the target I've put on his back.

CHAPTER FIVE

We tell students not to leave the path. To beware the dark. I break both rules as I stand here in the shadows of the Arts Pavilion, prowling among the bushes like a burglar. I peer through the window into Dagursson's office, seeking ideas, additional weapons, and the excuse that'll get me close enough to kill him.

I need to get in, do the deed, and get out.

I'd failed Charlotte, but I won't fail Annelise. If killing the old Viking is the only way to keep her alive, then that's what I'll do. Even though it might very well mean my own death.

I hold my breath, watching as he rises and walks to his bookshelves. But instead of selecting a book, he reaches his index finger high. Presses something. A panel pops open.

A secret hiding spot.

What does he keep in there? Is that where he's tucked away the information about my family? If I could actually track them down… The possibilities make me reel. I could take Annelise to them. We could flee; they'd give us shelter. We could make a fresh start.

Discovering how to open it is suddenly in the top five on

my life's priority list. I wrench my neck, squinting, but can't detect any levers or buttons in this darkness and inch to the side for a better angle. A branch snaps underfoot. I hold my breath.

But the old vampire continues in his own world. He hasn't heard me—he wouldn't. The thick masonry of the Arts building is as soundproof as a fortress. It'll conceal my approach. Because I act tonight. No matter what.

I'd have liked more time to plan, but this is my only window when I'm certain to be alone. I dropped my students at various points along the western coast of the island. Annelise will be busy trekking across the island. Between the rocky terrain and the bloodthirsty Draug roaming the countryside, even someone as talented as she is will be occupied trying to make her way back.

I push thoughts of her from my head. Focus. Only focus will get me out of here alive. Only my focus will save her.

Carefully, I check the urumi wrapped around my waist. It's the rarest of concealed weapons—one part coiling sword, one part whip—that I wear like a belt, hidden until the last moment. It's the most dangerous blade ever created, as likely to kill me as it is to behead any vampire.

And yet, in my pocket is something I'm banking Dagursson will find even more threatening: a simple plastic lighter. By the time he knows what's happening, I'll have my urumi wrapped around his throat and a flame threatening his scrolls. It'll be enough, I hope, to make him tell me what he knows about my remaining family.

I take the handle of the urumi in my hand. It's cold, and I grip harder, imagining my heart as cold as this steel. I flex my hand, pumping blood into my fingers.

I watch the vampire pull out a scroll. He shuts the panel again and walks slowly back to his desk. His feet find the way by rote, so completely immersed is he in his reading.

I will kill Dagursson. Preserve Annelise.

It's all the courage I need. Slowly, I extract the coiled blade.

Guard Annelise. Behead Dagursson.

Forget subterfuge and strategy. I'll storm in and surprise him, whipping my blade before he thinks to look up. Paper-thin steel will bite his flesh, bringing hundreds of years of walking this earth to a dead stop.

I stalk from the bushes. A shadow moves on the path. I freeze. I'd know the curve of those shoulders anywhere.

"Bloody hell." I've only murmured under my breath, but I'm heard.

Annelise stops, turns, steps closer.

I tear into her the moment she's within earshot and hiss into the darkness. "What are you doing here?"

Even in the shadows, I sense her recoil. "Hi to you, too, Ronan."

I take my urumi into my left hand and grab her arm with my right, tugging her back onto the path. "How'd you get back so fast?" She shuffles close, her side bumping mine. I experience a stupid, pleased sensation and shove it away again. "You should be halfway across the island right about now."

"Why, thank you, Ronan," she says in a voice thick with sarcasm. "I think I did a great job, too. It's all that stuff I learned about the Draug. They feed on fear, and seeing as I'm not scared of them anymore, they're not hungry when I'm around." She stops walking when I pause to wrap the urumi back around my waist. "I mean, except for that time I was covered in my own blood. Being covered in your own blood would make"—she stopped short, tuning into what I was doing—"what the *hell* is that?"

"It's a weapon," I say quietly.

"Thanks, Sherlock. I mean what kind?" She tentatively reaches out to touch the blade. Her fingers brush mine.

I clench my jaw. "Careful."

"Does this…this"—she peers closer—"this *most awesome* object have anything to do with the fact that we're whispering?" At that, she tilts her head up and pins me with her eyes. She's closer to me than I realized.

I step away, beginning a brisk walk down the path. "Why are you here?"

She falls into step with a sigh. "I was looking for you."

I raise my eyebrows. "Why?" I know I'm being harsher than is necessary, but I'm in uncharted depths.

"I told you before," she says, frowning. "I have to talk to you." A hint of vulnerability edges her voice—a needful thing suggesting she requires me and only me.

Or maybe that's just my wishful thinking.

Either way, I have to stop short. Look down. Focus on getting the cursed urumi back in place without severing a finger.

She pauses beside me. "But it seems you have something to tell me first."

My head shoots up. "Tell you?" Have I betrayed my feelings so quickly?

"Yes, you have *got* to tell me the name of your weapon. Are you"—she leans closer—"are you wearing it like a belt?" She's gleeful and adorable, and for an agonizing moment I contemplate a world in which she'd get to be gleeful about normal things like new shoes and good movies. It's a world I can't even imagine.

"It's called an urumi," I say tightly.

"An oo-whatie?"

"Urumi."

She shudders elaborately, an endearing pout wrinkling her face.

I know I'm supposed to be stern, but I decide not to fight my smile for her. "What's with the look?"

"Whips." She nods to the urumi. "They make me think of Masha," she says, referring to her longtime enemy, now dead.

"Yeesh."

"Technically it's not a whip. Think of it like a curling sword." I pull it back out, offering it to her. "Go ahead. You can hold it. Be careful, though. People have been known to slice their noses off while swinging it."

"Nice," she says, hefting the weapon in her hands. "Where on earth did it come from?"

"India."

She gives me that look I know so well. "No, dummy, I mean where did *you* get it?"

I pause. I could lie, but what would be the point? Annelise and I are way past lying.

I lead her to a bend in the path obscured by hedges. When I face her again, only the faintest starlight remains, glimmering along her cheekbone, casting her mouth in half light, half shadow.

"It was my sister's weapon," I say quietly. All Acari are assigned a weapon, something in tune with who they are. Annelise has her throwing stars. Masha had a whip. Charlotte got an urumi—though I never understood why. My wee sister with something so lethal never clicked for me.

Annelise gives my comment the weighty pause it deserves. Finally, she asks, "And you know how to use it?"

"Who do you think trained Masha?"

"Ronan. Well now." The look she gives me is a considering once-over, an assessment, like a girl seeing a guy in a new light. "I had no idea."

I stand taller. Because I'm a piteous idiot. "There's much you don't know."

Like how I might be going off to my death in order to protect her.

I gird myself to meet her eyes again. She's watching me pensively. She's so much smaller than me, but she's so close. It'd be so easy to lean down. To angle just so.

"I have a secret to tell you," she says quietly.

Her words stab me. Sharp emotion hews me like a chisel through ice. Does she have the same thoughts I do? Thoughts of how all I want is for us to touch. Not with my powers—just a normal touch, taking her hands in mine. How easy it would be to lean over, to close the gap between us. To bring my mouth to hers.

"A secret?" My voice is a harsh rasp. Might she be having thoughts like mine right now?

"Emma's alive," she says. "That's what I wanted to tell you."

CHAPTER SIX

"What?" I turn and walk to a crook in the path where I stand and stare into the trees, hiding my face from her. I need a moment to make sense of her words. Her secret isn't that she loves me. Of course it isn't. I'm a fool.

She follows, and so I busy myself with the urumi, taking it from her. I nick my palm getting it back around my waist. "This better not be any more of that nonsense about you breaking into the castle," I say finally. "The vampires—"

"No, Ronan. Listen. I did it. I snuck inside the keep."

My insides seize the moment the words come out of her mouth. Slowly, I meet her gaze. "What did you say?"

My expression must be dangerous because she recoils slightly. "It's okay," she says quickly. "I'm fine. It's just…I did it. I snuck inside the keep."

"How?" How could she have done such a thing and survived? Many girls went into that castle—and until now, none have come back out.

"I broke in." She waves it away, her expression urgent, desperate with some other news. "That's not the point. The point is, I think Emma is alive."

I grow still, uncertain I've heard correctly. Emma was

her best friend, and Annelise still blames herself for her death. "Did you see her?"

She shakes her head. "No, but—"

I interrupt at once. Hope is a dangerous thing on this island, cutting more deeply than any esoteric sword. I should know. "Emma is dead, Annelise."

"No," she says firmly, "just listen. That's what I needed to tell you. I think she might be alive. There were other Acari there. They were drugged—at least, I think they were. They were shuffling around, all dead eyed, like Stepford girls or something. And Frost—oh God—my roommate Frost was there, too. On a *table*, Ronan. Laid out on a table. It was so creepy. She looked willing, as though it was some great honor. And then a woman came in—a *woman*, Ronan—a vampire woman. She took out this knife, and she… The boys they…" Her face cracks then, her knees beginning to fold beneath her.

I reach out and wrap one arm around her, then the other. Before I know it, I've tucked her close. She nestles perfectly into place. I shush her, murmuring, "It's okay. I can imagine what they did. You don't have to tell me."

She pushes away. "No, Ronan. You *can't* imagine. It's horrific. There's this ritual…where they…they…"

She's shivering now, and I rub my hands along her arms. "Breathe, Ann. Remember our tactical breathing," I coax, knowing the comment might interrupt her spiral. Tactical breathing: inhaling, holding, exhaling on a four count. She'd given me such grief about the absurd term, but it didn't matter—tactical breathing was made for situations like this.

But apparently whatever the vampires did to Frost was too gruesome to recount, because once she gathers herself, she takes a different tack. "They have all the dead Acari's weapons hanging on the walls," she begins evenly. "But Frost was still alive, at least she was at first, and her weapon, that ridiculous ax, was lying on a table. And they had Emma's

Buck knife on the table, too. As though she was next or something. As though she's still alive."

She gives me a pleading look. I know that look. Every alarm in my head shrills to life.

"I have to save her," she says. "Don't you see? Emma is alive. She has to be."

"Promise you won't do anything without me." What if I die trying to assassinate Dagursson, and she goes back into that keep alone to save her friend? My hands tighten around her arms. "Promise you won't go it alone."

"Who would help me? Who could I even trust? I mean, yeah, there's you, and Carden—"

"Don't tell him what you just told me," I snap. Carden claims he loves her—and God help me, I believe him—but I also believe he loves his crusade at least as much. I fear the day will come when he places his own objectives before anything—or anyone—else. "Don't confide in Carden. Not yet."

"He's not one of them," she says instantly. "I know that."

"But he's a vampire. And that *I* know."

Her face hardens as she processes something. "Well, then, how about the female vampire thing. Did you know that, too? You didn't exactly flinch when I said it."

That's my Ann. Always knowing, always guessing. That's how I know she'll survive after I'm gone.

I've taken too long to answer her, and my silence betrays me.

"No way," she practically shouts, then catches herself, continuing in an angry whisper. "You have got to be kidding me. Women can be vampires, and you knew, and you didn't tell me?"

"The Vampire Directorate likes to keep it a secret," I say.

"Secrets, secrets, so many secrets."

I know there's something I should say here, something she needs to hear, but I'm too blinded by my own questions.

"Was it Sonja?"

"Wait, you even know her name?" She deflates at that. "Yes, the vampire's name was Sonja. And doesn't it just suck for me that the person I trust most didn't even tell me something so ginormous?"

I'm the one she trusts the most? "I didn't know she was on the island," I manage, fighting the urge to pull her close.

She's scowling hard now, and I can see it's to quell some intense emotion. "So that leaves…let's see…*nobody*. There's nobody else I can trust. I'm alone. Everyone I trusted is dead." A light enters her eye, and she meets my gaze in earnest. "Do you think I could trust Alcántara? He was in the keep, but it was weird, he—"

"Kenzie," I blurt, grasping onto anything to interrupt that train of thought. "There's always Kenzie," I repeat, recalling her dorm Proctor. "On this island, having friends is dangerous. But allies, they're a good thing. She could be your ally."

She scowls. "Spare me the lecture."

"Just listen." I can't have her thinking about Alcántara. "Kenzie is different from the others," I insist. "I know. I was the one who brought her in."

She jerks from me. "Why are you always going on about Kenzie?"

My hands are left cold and empty. I clench them into fists. "What?"

"*What* what? I mean, *what* is the big deal with Kenzie?"

I struggle to parse this sudden hostility. "It's just a sense I get."

"You've told me to trust her before. I don't see what makes you say it. Kenzie, Kenzie, Kenzie. What's so special about her?"

I smile then, broadly. Am I seeing what I think I'm seeing? Once more, I reach for her. She flinches at first, but I won't be stopped. I cup her cheeks in my hands, making her face me. "Kenzie and I aren't close like you and I are, if that's what you're afraid of."

"I'm not afraid of anything," she says quickly.

"Good. Because you have no cause to be," I say. "Kenzie is nothing to me. You are…" *Everything*, I long to say. *You are everything.* "She's nothing to me, but you are. Trust me."

"I do trust you." She gives me a smile. It wavers but it's genuine. I see relief on her face, and it settles something in my heart. "I just said so, didn't I?"

I'd mentioned Kenzie, and she got jealous. That says something big. Something significant. I carefully set aside the thought to consider when I'm alone.

"Now do *you* trust *me*?" she asks.

I might've instantly said yes, but she uses an extra-sweet tone that puts me on guard. "Um, aye?"

She falls into me, curling her fists into the front of my jacket to give a little jiggle, and it just about slays me. "Then please tell me, Ronan. Pleeaase. Why do you have that supercool weapon?"

I can't get her involved. Slowly, regretfully, I settle my armor back into place. "I have my reasons," I say in a blank voice.

She isn't having it. "Mmhmm." She crosses her arms at her chest. "I've told you all my secrets. When will you tell me yours?"

"How's *never* work for you?"

A joyful crack of a laugh escapes her, and she slaps a hand over her mouth. "Ronan! A smile and now a joke. I can't believe it. Did someone come and switch bodies with you?" Her hands are still on my jacket, and she pats my chest.

She's merely playing, but I stop breathing. No armor is strong enough for this.

But she's seen what she does to me. She's read my expression as only someone who knows me could. She stiffens, too. We each take a small step apart.

"Tell me," she whispers.

I no longer know what we're talking about.

And so I address the only thing I know how. Death. "There's something I have to do."

"You mean someone you need to kill," she says, perceptive as always.

"There will be a big change soon." A member of the Vampire Directorate murdered—it's unheard of. "A seismic change," I stress. "Things could get strange for a while."

"Good thing I'll have you around," she says, fishing for a response I can't give.

What she doesn't know is there's a very big chance I won't be around. To assassinate a vampire that powerful—it'd be a miracle to come out alive. "You must be careful," is all I tell her.

But she's heard the unspoken message. I'm in danger.

Everything about her sharpens, hardens, and I get a sense of what it is her opponents face in the ring—what it is the other girls fear. "You're going to do something." She looks back the way we came, and even though the path is obscured, the roof of the Arts Pavilion rises above the hedges, its tiles taking on a ghostly glow in the starlight. "In there." She knows who works in that building. Dagursson *is* the Arts building.

"True," I say blandly.

She faces me, her eyes challenging, waiting. But I don't elaborate.

"Whatever, Ronan." She turns from me. "If you're not going to talk to me, I'm heading back."

I'm losing her. "Ann. Look at me."

She turns slightly, and I study her profile, trying to read the peculiar expression there.

"Is it that I called you Ann?" I ask. "Do you not like when I call you that?"

"No." She shrugs, looking pained. "I…actually…I like it.

A lot." She shifts, facing me once more. "What I don't like is the feeling you're keeping stuff from me. Like, how can I possibly believe I know you when you're like a steel vault?"

But she does know me. She sees me as no other person ever has. I realize how lonely I've been—how much I've needed her, needed the way she just seems to get it, to get me. Perhaps it's how she got past my defenses. How she found her way into my heart.

But I can't tell her that, and so I'll tell her everything else. I want to keep her safe, but she's too smart to be kept in the dark.

"I fight in secret," I confess, "against the Directorate."

"Seriously?" Her eyes go wide, as I knew they would.

I nod. "And I've been ordered to kill Dagursson."

"Tonight?" Her voice catches on the word. "You're doing that right now?"

As she says it, I know. It won't happen tonight. Annelise is here now, with me. There would be tomorrow to deal with Dagursson. But how many more tomorrows would I get with her? "Not tonight."

I play a dangerous game—I suffer no illusions on that count. One day soon will be my last. The time will come when I see her, and it'll be the last time I do.

Have I already touched her for the last time? I fist my hands tighter to keep my arms fixed like boards at my side.

"I figured something like that was going on," she says. Her wide-eyed stare has been replaced by the shrewd Ann I know so well.

"You guessed?"

"No, not exactly. I just figured you're too…too…good to be bad. If that makes any sense."

I find myself smiling. "I'm good, is it?"

"You know, in a bad way, of course." Her own smile fades, and she tenses as a truth hits her. "Before I showed up, you were going to go in there and kill Dagursson. You were going in, and you probably wouldn't have come out, and then I'd never see you again."

I nod, unable to speak. Her thoughts have mirrored my own, and it knocks me flat.

"Let me help you," she says in sudden earnest. "We can do this together. We're a team, Ronan."

The sentiment is a balm, and yet I give a single sharp shake to my head. "I won't risk your life." What I won't tell her is how I'm doing this precisely to preserve hers.

"My life..." Her arms flail. "What's that without you?"

I mean something to her. Could it even be possible?

My eyes go to her lips. I step closer. What is this thing between us? What would it feel like to let ourselves go? To pretend our lives were different, that the smallest of our decisions didn't have deadly consequences?

She opens her mouth but hesitates. "What are you thinking?" She speaks in a wondering tone, as awed and confounded as I.

"I'm thinking..." Again, my eyes go to her mouth. I'm thinking I might not survive the week. I'm thinking I'd like to kiss her before I die. But I won't make something happen that she doesn't want. She has Carden to consider, and so I must be sure. "Are you afraid?"

She shifts. Did she just edge closer?

"There are things I'm afraid of when you're around," she says, "and it's not this."

What does that mean? If it's going to end soon for me, I can't do it with this hanging over my head. This feeling. This unasked question. I must know what it's like to kiss her.

There's nothing to stop us. Not even Carden could avenge me for taking a simple kiss—not when I'm dead from my attempt to kill Dagursson.

And what *of* Carden? She shares a blood bond with him—a vampire of tremendous power—and, yet, even that isn't enough to stop this thing between us.

But does she want it, too?

Her hand grazes mine. She *has* edged closer. Her eyes are steady on mine. She does want this.

I have to seize it. To take what might be this one last pleasure. To answer this one last question.

To take this one kiss.

Slowly, I lean down. I touch my mouth to hers.

They say the world stops when you experience something this pure, this shatteringly true. But as I kiss Annelise the world doesn't stop at all.

Rather, for the first time I can remember, I can breathe again.

CHAPTER SEVEN

Striding to the breakfast the next day, I'm a man reborn. I can face anything. Anyone. Dagursson, Alcántara, Carden… Bring it on.

Bring it on. It's something Annelise would say. Her spirit has infused me that fully, touched me that deeply. I'll make her mine completely. I'll find a way.

With the thought, I spot the Scottish vampire heading toward me on the path. Does he know about Annelise and me? Did he feel something from afar, stirring in her heart as we kissed? Does he know it was me?

I pull back my shoulders and pick up my pace. I can face anyone…*especially* Carden McCloud.

Maybe Annelise has already told him. She told him she feels something for me, and he's come to confront me. I meet his focused glare and don't look away.

But as our paths cross, the only thing he has to say to me is, "Best hurry, pup."

"Hurry?" It takes me a moment to process that his scowl has nothing to do with Annelise. As pleasant as it is to imagine confrontations with my rival, it's time to get out of my head.

"Aye, lad. Hurry. As in shake a leg. Get cracking. However you toddlers say it. Freya wants Dagursson dead. Or have you forgotten?"

I grit my teeth. "No, Master McCloud. I've not forgotten." I'm so not in the mood for his vampiric condescension.

He cuffs me on the shoulder. "No need to 'Master' me, pup. You know I find the customs of Hugo and his lads to be a load of shite." He swings an easy arm around my shoulders and pulls me into a walk. "I'm only wanting to know why Alrik is still walking about." The shift in his tone is subtle, but I hear it like the blast of a foghorn—he's serious.

"It's not that simple. I had to stake him out first." And then kiss your girlfriend.

"Time to stop staking out and just start staking." He jostles me with a good humor I know is counterfeit.

I stop short, spinning to face him. "And what if I do my part and fail?" I've played it out in my mind dozens of times. Who knows, maybe I'll manage to kill the old Viking, but it's hard to imagine walking away from it alive. "As long as I do my part, do you swear she'll live?"

He stares at me a moment. The way he weighs my words tells me his answer will be honest. I might not trust that we have the same goals, but Carden is driven, ultimately, by the older ways, the righteous and noble. I believe his word, once given, is good. It's just how he is.

"Yes, pup," he says finally. "You've my word." He begins walking again, a pleasant strolling gait belying the fact that we were just casually discussing my likely demise. "Just get on with it, aye? Here's the situation: if you don't kill Dagursson soon, Freya will be forced to kill Drew. And if that happens, well, I'll have no choice but to turn around and kill you, and that'd be a real pisser, eh? We'll all be upset if it comes to that.... Well, just me, actually, as I'll be the last one standing. Which means that after I kill you, I'll have to slay the old Viking myself, and that'll put me in a foul temper for certain."

I pick up my pace. "You could always just cut to the chase and kill me now—isn't that what you vampires do?" I force a smile but my voice is steel.

"Don't tempt me." He smiles, too. Our jousting is playful. Sort of. "You know I'm not as bloodthirsty as my vampire colleagues."

No need when you have Annelise to feed on.

The thought churns my belly to acid. "As you say," I manage. I quicken my step. I've got to get away from him before my fist cracking on his jaw turns from fantasy to reality.

"Why the rush?" His hand seizes my shoulder, stopping me. "I'm feeling…avoided." His words ooze that easy Carden charm, but I know him well enough to sense the threat rippling beneath.

He knows something is up. Curiously, it seems he doesn't know about Annelise and me. Which isn't to say he doesn't suspect something.

I flinch away. "Not avoiding you at all." I shoot a casual look in the direction of the dining hall. Annelise will be there already, maybe even waiting for me. "I'm simply hungry." Though it's not food I crave.

Carden sends a considering glance to the dining hall then back to me. "I'll reckon our wee Drew is there, eating her brekkie." He speaks casually, but I've learned his nonchalance is its own weapon. "Tell me, pup. Is she worth the trouble?"

Always. My desire to see her surges at the thought. She is always ever worth it.

But I only shrug, keeping a careful handle on my own nonchalance. "Annelise?" I say offhandedly. "She's no trouble. Why do you ask?"

"Slaying Dagursson is very nearly suicide." He gives a

considered shake to his head. "Which means you're risking your hide to protect a girl who's already bonded to another." His quicksilver laugh is part humor, part reminder. "So either you're a sucker for punishment or maybe just a sucker, eh?" His eyes narrow on me, seeking, probing. Does he suspect how deeply my true feelings run? "Listen, lad. I wish you no ill will. I've been around a long time. Long enough to know you need to seize what peace you can. This thing—you staying to fight on the Isle—it won't bring your sister back. Drew isn't Charlotte. You've got nothing to gain. Even now, you could be on *Eilean Ban-Laoch*, maybe having some sweet thing peel grapes for you, eh? Or paddling about in the surf as you do." He gives me a friendly jostle. "Just do what you can to be happy. It's something I've learned from our wee Drew. Why do you make it so hard for yourself? Pleasures are rare—it's important to seize what you can. Freya would give you anything if she thought you were her creature through and through."

"You mean if I followed her every whim without question?" I shrug it off, this moment between Carden and me. "I work for Freya. I don't worship her."

"You do more than work for her; you've a pact with her. A devil's bargain—isn't that what they call it? You've made a deal but get naught in return." He gives a considering pause. "But that can't be true, can it? We all want something. And I keep trying to figure what it is you get from all this. You say you want to protect Annelise, but you know I've got that covered. Maybe you just want to stay on *Eyja næturinnar* because you want to figure out how to make a vampire of yourself. Is that it?"

I speak before I think. "Not hardly." I soften the words with a laugh.

Carden doesn't smile with me, though. Instead, an uncharacteristically serious look crosses his face. "I want you to admit something."

I brace for it. Now will he ask about Annelise?

"Your power," he says. "Can you use it on vampires?" His words come easy, but his vivid gaze is pinned on me. "Will you be able to use it on Dagursson?"

It's something I've wondered a thousand times, and the answer is, I don't know. I suppose it'll be tested soon enough…when I face Dagursson.

But as I begin to reply, I spot a glint in Carden's eye—a hunger to know the strengths and weaknesses of someone who might become as much enemy as ally. "No," I lie. "I can't use it on vampires."

"Then Godspeed, my man." He gives a very Carden-like shake of his head, both apology and amusement. "I expect Dagursson to be dead by the end of the week. Or…"

"Or I will be?"

But his attention moves over my shoulder. He claps a hand to his chest as a broad smile spreads across his face. "And here I thought the sun rose in the east."

I turn. It's her. Annelise.

She looks from him, to me, and back again. I suppose he is a vampire—her bonded vampire—and I suppose it *is* wise to give such a creature your full attention, and yet I can't help the jealousy that roils through me. She belongs to him.

For now.

"Acari Drew," I greet her formally.

"Tracer Ronan," she replies with a studied detachment that hollows my chest. Is this her being afraid? Does she worry how her bond might betray her feelings?

I stiffen, poised to protect her in case of the worst. But Carden doesn't seem to sense anything. Instead, he pulls her into his arms, drags his fingers through her hair, and tips her face to his. Now he's kissing her forehead.

I have to look away. Is he doing this for my benefit? Marking his territory like a dog?

I sense more nuzzling, then he proclaims, "'She walks in

beauty, like the night. Of cloudless climes and starry skies; And all that's best of dark and bright.'"

"You have got to be kidding me," I mutter.

But he heard me. I think maybe I wanted him to. "What's the problem, boy? Not a fan of poetry?"

"Poetry." I give a dismissive scowl. As if this isn't secretly killing me.

Carden says I should try to be happy? Fine, I know what'll make me happy: Annelise. She is the pleasure I'll seize.

"That's a poem?" Annelise asks. There's a whiff of wonderment in her voice that makes me bristle.

I study her, the way the morning light hits her at an angle. Her hair has darkened this long winter, now yellow from a yellowish white. Beauty like the night? Annelise is more than that—she's like the sun.

"Oh, aye, I'm full of surprises. That was Lord Byron." Carden turns to Annelise. "He lived life…what is it you say?"

She shifts her weight. Balancing herself or trying subtly to pull away? I can't tell. "He lived large?"

Carden's laugh is joyful and heartfelt. "Aye, just so."

I want to impale the bastard then and there. My wrists flex automatically, feeling the handmade stakes I keep ever hidden beneath my sleeves.

"You'd better get to the dining hall before the good stuff goes," Annelise tells me. There's a look of alarm on her face—she's seen my gesture, just as she's seen my secret stakes before.

She's trying to get rid of me. I've been a fool. I begin to shutter my emotions.

But then her hand darts to mine and squeezes. "I'll find you, Ronan. Later." Intensity lights her eyes in a secret message.

She's changed me. And I'll change everything for her. But first, she'll need time. She's the one who cheated on a vampire—she's probably all kinds of anxious.

I carry a warmth hidden in my heart, reserved for her alone. I free it now, Carden be damned. I free it into the light of day, letting it fill my eyes as I return her gaze full on. *I'm here,* it says silently. *I wait. Forever if need be.* The sentiment I give voice to, though, is significantly more banal. "What, precisely, do you characterize as the good stuff? Would that be tinned oats or expired yogurt?"

She understands. Knows I won't pressure her. I imagine I'm the only one able to see her relief; it relaxes the set of her shoulders, eases something that had become pinched around her eyes. "Blood pudding," she answers with a shudder.

"A delicacy," Carden says, yet again inserting himself. He'll always be there, inserting himself. He's undead.

I can't have her yet, but I can protect her. I'll do this thing. In the end, I forgo the dining hall. Today, I decide. Not tonight but *today* I assassinate Dagursson. Perhaps Carden is right—perhaps it will kill me. I have no choice. All I know is I must keep Annelise safe.

CHAPTER EIGHT

I burst into the Arts Pavilion and head straight for Dagursson's office. At first I wanted to do this for Annelise, but now? Now I'm doing it for *us*.

I'll appease Freya by killing the vampire, and then, if Ann wishes it, she and I can run away. We could go wherever she desires. I'll find us a new place. I could find my family—Dagursson knows where they are. We could stay with them. It'd be on a faraway island where the sun shines. I only need to get the information from the vampire before I kill him.

I reach his door and pull back my shoulders. I wondered how to kill him, which ruse I could use to get inside, but in the end, my only plan is that there is no plan—there's no cover story clever enough to prevent the old Viking from suspecting me. And so I've got my urumi around my waist, stakes up my sleeves, and an old lighter in my pocket. My only hope is to take him by surprise.

I flex one hand as the other finds the lighter, my thumb poising on its small steel spinner. I'll threaten his scrolls. He'll tell me of my family. I'll find them, and they'll give us shelter.

Briefly, I seek inside myself, reaching for my power. I

don't summon it, not yet, in case the vampire is able to sense it, too. Maybe it won't be enough. Maybe it'll kill me.

Annelise. Her name is mantra in my head. *For us.*

I shove the door, and it opens with a *slam*. I'm powerful, driven. I'm a knight of old, storming the castle.

"Tracer," the vampire shouts, scolding. "Does Alcántara not teach manners to his errand boys?" He thinks I've been sent by another vampire. Of course he would. He's too arrogant to believe a mere mortal would think to take him on. It's a perfect ruse—it'll buy me time.

"Insolence, all around," he mutters. "The moment we let go of the ancient ways, we open the door to corruption and dishonor."

I scan the room, assessing his position without even thinking. He's seated at an old rolltop writing desk—legs tucked under, shoulders hunched over. The old Viking is impossibly fast but would need to move around furniture to get to me. Maybe it'll be enough to slow him. Maybe it won't.

"Well?" He puts down his pen and stares. "Tell me what the Spaniard wants so I can get back to my translations."

I walk straight to the far corner of the room. He tracks my gaze, sees what I see. The thing he values above all other things. What he'd do anything to protect. His scrolls, several of them, stacked on a nearby table. Threatening them is my only shot at answers. Will it be enough to make him speak?

Dagursson gapes in disbelief when I reach his worktable. "Whatever Alcántara wants, I assure you, it's not there. Does he have a message for me or not?" He heaves a put-out sigh and scoots back his chair.

"Alcántara," I say quickly, "says no need to get up for the fool boy."

He leans back, bemused by this unexpected reply. "Would the 'fool boy' care to explain?"

I'm at the table. It's time. I graze my power with an

invisible touch.

His eyes shrink to slits in his desiccated face. I sent a pulse of my power, and he felt it. I have to bite back an astonished grin. This changes everything.

"What game are you playing?" Dagursson's gaze flicks to his scrolls, suspicious now. "Don't tell me Hugo has developed a sudden taste for reading."

I grab one at random. "He wanted me to get this."

Dagursson shoots to his feet. "What does he want with the Normandy scroll? Does he…" But my lighter is in place, dancing beneath the ancient parchment. The instant he spots it, he bares his fangs in a hiss. He seems to grow, to rise, his energy looming over me, making it hard to breathe.

My heart slams in my chest. *Annelise, Annelise, Annelise*, it repeats with every beat. *Whatever happens, this is for you.* "Move and it burns," I tell him. The steadiness in my voice amazes me.

"What dirty, petty, childish trickery is the Spaniard up to now?" His eyes are brighter than any flame, riveted to my hand. "I tire of his political games."

He's stuck on this idea that I'm only here at Alcántara's behest. Though it's the thing keeping me alive at the moment, the assumption that I'm incapable of my own motivations rankles. He'll see.

He shifts, and I shout, "Stop," the word a harsh scrape in my throat. I ease the lighter closer to the scroll, close enough to make the tan parchment glow golden. "Sit down. I have questions."

"*You* have questions? You don't ask questions. And you don't…order…me." There's a ripple in the air—the mere sense of motion before it's even visible. He's leaping toward me.

I don't hesitate. I kiss flame to scroll. The thin, ancient parchment lights instantly. A warm, sweet smell, like incense, fills the room. I toss it in the bin and snatch up another scroll at once, daring him to move. “Sit or I light this one, too.”

Dagursson roars. But he’s stopped, just on the other side of the table.

“Sit,” I repeat, shouting to be heard. The scroll is crumpled in my fist. It’s close enough to the flame that I smell it. “I could burn these all day. So back up and sit down.”

Already I’ve made it further than I thought I would. I could survive this—survive to be with Annelise. I think of her, summon my strength. I’ve never stretched like this before. I reach deep for my power, repeating her name in my mind like a mantra. *Annelise.*

I think of her as I draw my power, and an internal dam breaks. Sensations swamp me. The taste of metal floods my mouth. A chill ripples the back of my neck. And, above all, a darkness beckons, just out of reach—my power, not truly touched before this moment. But I feel the vastness of it yawning within me at my core. It’s immeasurable. Terrifying. Seductive.

Dagursson grows silent. “Ah, you use your powers.” He purses his lips and shuts his eyes, inhaling dramatically. “How thrilling.”

The parchment smolders in the small trash can, and I wave the other scroll over it. “Now sit back down or I toss this one in the bin, too.”

He gives me an ominously blank stare. “Don’t think just because you’re Alcántara’s pet I’ll show you mercy.”

I shrug. “I imagine you wouldn’t.”

He glares down at his feet, as if he might find an answer there. “You’re using your tricks. On me.”

“Looks that way. Now sit.” I impart the command with every ounce of force at my disposal.

He pauses, seeming to fight it for a moment, but then, with a courtly nod of concession, he returns to his desk. He begins to shuffle his papers into neat stacks, as though I’ve merely interrupted his work rather than breaking protocol in the most radical of ways. "Did Hugo help you refine that little trick?" he asks finally. "You still haven't told me what he thinks to accomplish here." He adds under his breath, "Only a coward sends a child to do his business."

"I'm the one asking questions here." It's not an answer, but I need to continue to play along with his suspicions. I'll eventually run out of scrolls to burn, but if Dagursson thinks I have knowledge of treachery within the Vampire Directorate, maybe that'll be enough to get him talking. "I'd like some information."

"What information could you need or understand?" His voice reeks of condescension. "You're a child."

"Yeah, a child with a lighter." I flick it again and enjoy seeing him flinch. He didn't expect this. He thinks I fear him. He's wrong. "*Now* are you ready?"

"You think fire will make me speak?"

"No." I walk toward him. I dig deep now, deeper even than before. I touch his shoulder and feel a burst of power, like a magnet jumping to meet its opposite pole. "I think *I'll* make you speak."

He hisses in a breath, and it feels like triumph.

I put the lighter down. "Put your hands behind your back." I slide the urumi from around my waist, and his eyes light with recognition.

"Charlotte's weapon." His smile is overly familiar.

"Don't say her name," I snap.

He watches, utterly still, as I wrap the coiled blade around his chest. It doesn't exactly tie him to the chair, but if he tried to move, he'd certainly sever something vital. "Are you going to torture me, boy?" His voice is bland, matter-of-fact.

"Nah." I stroll around him. "You'd probably enjoy that, you old freak."

"It stands to reason, I suppose." He shrugs, as if we're

debating music theory instead of sadism. "Hugo would be here himself if that were the intention. He's not one to miss such spectacle."

"I could make this painless, Alrik. You just need to answer one question." When I reach the front of the chair again, I lean down, staring him in the face. This close, his skin is an intricate map of creases and hollows. He is ancient…and soon he'll be dead. "Who is this family of mine, and where do they live?"

"Ahhhh." He emits a slow sigh, his face parting into a lizard's smile. "I see what this is all about."

"No tricks. No chatting. Let's just get on with it, shall we?" I extend my arms, revealing the homemade stakes concealed under the sleeves of my sweater. I remove one and touch it just over his heart. "I brought more than just a lighter."

"An old-fashioned stake. How quaint. You made that?" He peers up and meets my blank expression. "Clever boy. I warn you, though. You must be exact. Even with your powers, such a stake will do no good unless it's placed with absolute precision. Can you do that? Can you find my heart with absolute precision?"

"We could find out right now," I say, pressing harder. "Or you can play nice and tell me where my family is."

"You modern children, you think you can have what you want the moment you want it."

I press the stake deeper, until I feel the bone beneath his skin. "So you *do* know how to find them."

"I know where one family member is." The sly, leering quirk to his mouth tells me he speaks the truth. "You can read it on your family's scroll." He purses his lips as if he's trying to hide a smirk. "Didn't you know? You have a family scroll. I hope you didn't burn it. What delicious irony that would be."

"Shut up." I glance back and scan the table, but the rolls

and rolls of paper all look the same. "Which one is it?"

"Aren't they lovely?" he says in a marveling sort of voice. "The oldest ones are papyrus. Made from reeds grown in the Nile Delta. Now that was a fascinating era—would that I could've seen it firsthand."

I go to the table and run my hand along them. "Which one?" I repeat in a snarl. I'm running out of time.

"Remove your hand, if you please," he snaps. "The oils of human skin are very damaging."

My fist curls around the nearest scroll. It bears drawings of fruits and birds that don't seem relevant to me, and so I squeeze and toss the crumpled ball into the trash bin. "That's what I think of your papers. Now tell me where you keep the information about my family."

"Savage," he mutters. With a nod to his bookshelf, he says, "As you wish. My most prized scrolls are in the safe."

I'm a prized scroll? The secret of my lineage just got bigger. I go to the bookshelf and run my hands along the sides of the wood, seeking a hidden button or lever. I'd watched him open the secret panel from afar, when I staked out his office. "How does this work?"

"Shall I show you?" The words hiss in my ear. Dagursson. Somehow he's gotten free, though it wasn't without cost—the metallic scent of his own blood clings to him.

"Cut yourself, did you?" I try to spin, but he's at my back, his talon fingers curling into my shoulder.

I hear the *shick* of metal—my urumi unfurling. He flicks his arm out, cracking it like a whip. The steel makes a dreadful singing hum that reverberates through his office. "What a treat," he says with delight. "They say the urumi is difficult to use, but I'm not finding this so hard at all." He shakes the blade out at his side and steel nicks the tops of my shoes, slicing the leather where it touches. I must've stiffened under his grip because he says, "Shall we play together, you and I?"

"Back off," I say, reaching once more for my power. And for a moment, I do feel it, in my blood, buzzing where his hand touches my body.

"Oh," he chirps. The bastard is toying with me. "Your talents are impressive indeed, Ronan. But I fear you've miscalculated. Sadly, you're just not powerful enough." A burst of cold emanates from his grip as he slams my chest into the shelf. Books topple around us, and the smell of mildew fills my sinuses. "Or maybe it's just your intellect that's lacking. It was very stupid, your coming in here. I believe I've been right all along to think that Charlotte got all the brains in your family."

"I told you not to say her name." I summon another burst of power. Enough to twist my body and propel myself away from the bookshelf, slamming a heel into his knee.

He loses his grip on me for a satisfying instant but is back on me immediately, angrier than ever. He spins me around, slamming my face into his books. "Temper," he growls. His hand is bitter cold on my neck. I feel the bones of his thin fingers, his razor-sharp nails, seeking, probing. He slides his thumb down along my shoulder, finds a spot, and presses hard. So hard it feels his nail might cut through my clothes, through my skin.

I try to flinch away. I want to open my mouth, but I can't make a sound. I'm paralyzed.

"That's right," he says, oozing a satisfied sigh. "They call this the baroreceptor reflex. Fascinating thing." He presses harder, and my vision dims. "If I were to hold this pose longer, you would eventually black out and die. But that's no fun."

I find myself swept into the chair where I'd just had him minutes before. He sat me down with my chest facing the chair back. He sweeps the urumi around my waist, binding me to the wood. "This is such an elegant little weapon," he says. And then he tears off my sweater, my shirt.

Blood is slowly pumping back into my brain. The chair back is padded, and its red velvet plushness against my chest is so out of place, it jars my senses fully alert. My eyes skitter across the room, looking for ideas, for a way out. Damn me for getting caught like this.

"You acted averse to torture," he says, "but perhaps you simply haven't experienced the finest hand." He rakes his fingers through my hair and wrenches my head up to face him. "You see, I can't let you die before I get some of my own questions answered."

He slaps me then, hard. Hard enough to make my eyes water.

I suck the blood from my teeth and spit onto his rug. "You going to slap me to death? Because if that's the case, I'll make myself more comfortable."

"Mind the carpet." He slams my face into the chair. "Now tell me who sent you."

"I'm here of my own choice. I've longed to take you down." It's a stupid thing to say, but if I'm going to die, I'll die speaking my mind. For once, I'll show them who I really am. I've suppressed the fight inside me. Relied on Annelise's grit to satisfy my longing to strike. But now it's my turn.

"I don't believe you're that complicated, Ronan. Who is behind this? If not Hugo, who?"

I can't let him discover Freya's part. My personal feelings for the female vampire aside, she's fighting for something I believe in. I won't betray the cause. "Trust me when I say I walk alone." It's the most honest thing I've said all night.

"Then you're a fool." He shakes his head, marveling. "Why would you dare such a transgression?"

If he thinks I'm just a fool, all the better to act the part. Anything to keep Ann out of this. I take a deep breath and flex—this is going to hurt. "I guess I've just never quite liked you, Alrik. I can call you Alrik, right? I mean, you're beating the shite out of me. Why rest on formality when you're beating the shite out of me?"

He slams the back of my head. "I do not"—slams again—"appreciate"—slam—"foul mouths."

It takes a moment to shake the clarity back into my head. "I can't help but notice you keep attacking from behind, Alrik. I thought you Vikings had more moves than that." I run my tongue along the inside of my mouth and spit out a piece of broken tooth. "Or are you just afraid to face me?"

"You'll see my moves," he says with a depraved little laugh.

I crane my neck, but he's disappeared behind me, and so I can only listen as he walks to his desk and rifles through drawers. At the sound of metal clanging, I bristle.

"I can smell your anxiety, young Tracer. Do you regret your actions? Perhaps if you'd known how to keep your attitude in check, this wouldn't have to be so very arduous for the both of us."

"Don't let me be a trouble to you," I say, dreading what's in store.

"Trouble indeed." He's back. When I try to see what he's brought from his desk that's making such an awful clatter, he merely shoves my face into the chair again. "I'm afraid we're in for a long afternoon. Unless you wish to inform?" There's more unnerving clattering behind me. "No? No matter. I have ways of changing your mind."

I hear the sound of a clasp springing open, like something on a small case. "You have a special kit for this?" I ask. My scoffing will only mean more pain for me later, but I need it now—anything to keep my wits. I think of Annelise again, this time with new insight, finally understanding why she's always so quick with a sarcastic barb. I let my own barbs rip now…for her. "Or was that just the sound of a wee chess set popping open? Though, actually, you seem more like a backgammon man. You going to challenge me to a match?"

"Your goading does you no credit, young Tracer. Alcántara has clearly lost control of you. It seems it's up to me to teach you a lesson." He runs a fingernail down my naked back, along my spine. "Have you heard of the Blood Eagle? It's a method of torture much favored in the Icelandic sagas."

He's at his case again, rifling about. He's selected something. I hear the whisper of metal sliding against leather—a dagger pulled from a sheath?

"Such a glorious thing," he says, once more at my back. "Modern historians believe the Blood Eagle is merely the stuff of fiction. The skaldic poems could be particularly, shall we say, fierce. But I was there, you'll recall. It was a time when fiction wasn't much more brutal than fact. Indeed, I've seen the Eagle performed with my own eyes. I've always wanted to try it."

A metal tip touches my skin. "The Norse ways were so much more than just crude sadism. We appreciated subtleties of metaphor, ones that transcend simple pain. Because true anguish goes beyond the mere physical, yes? It's a psychological state, something profound and moving."

With the lightest tickling touch, he traces his blade lightly down my spine. *Bump, bump*, over every rise and fall of each rib. "To perform the ritual properly, one must cut each rib by the spine. And then you splay them out into great wings. The lungs are revealed, of course, delicately flapping like an eagle's feathers. The effect is quite magnificent."

He sinks the tip of his blade into my skin and holds it there. "Shall we try it?" He twists the metal deeper. "Unless you wish to tell me who sent you? Who do you work for? Who do you protect?"

I pull in a deep breath—*Annelise…I would've liked to see you one more time*—and let it out with a great exhale. I've released more than just air from my body.

I am ready.

"I'd thought listening to you talk was the torture," I say blithely, while inside I brace for my own death.

Without pause, Dagursson slams down his hand. But as his knife hits my rib, it's deflected, dashed to the side, slicing under my skin instead, filleting me like a fish. I gasp, then bite down on my lips. I refuse to give him the satisfaction.

"Hurt?" He removes the blade from beneath my skin and taps the exposed bone.

"Oh, have we started?" I ask, managing to keep my voice calm. Annelise would've appreciated the line, I think.

I imagine her grief at my death. Carden will comfort her. He'll take care of her, and for that I'm grateful. The thought stabs more deeply than any blade. But I *am* grateful.

Instantly, he tries again, and this time he hits his mark. But still the bone doesn't snap. His knife has gone deep, though, and a warm wash of blood courses down my back.

I smell it, taste it, it's all around me. Rushing, pooling. I realize it's in my mouth, on my tongue, bitten from keeping quiet. I experience a jumble of sensations—the warmth of all that blood, but there's cool, too, in my head, tingling from its loss.

"You're right," he says. "We haven't really begun, Tracer. We will go all day. Unless you have something to say to me?"

"No," I say, but the word doesn't come out right. I clear my throat and begin again. "No," I repeat clearly, "not that I can think of."

"Shame." He has at me again, chiseling as if I'm a mound of stone. "Bone is so hard to crack. This will take several"—he strikes again—"more"—and again—"attempts."

I realize the pain is beginning to suck me in. *Focus.* I've trained for this. I mustn't lose control.

I concentrate on Annelise. Her face is the locus of my

meditation as I systematically imagine each part of my body, forcing it to relax, to melt away. My self—the essence that is me—gradually recedes until I'm no longer my body. My body has become mere flesh, apart from my mind. It is what's being tortured—not me.

I compartmentalize my mind. The rational part—the one reserved for escape—races, seeking a way out. I scrutinize Dagursson's every move. Somewhere, my chance awaits—there's always a chance. I just need to know it when I see it.

As for the rest of my mind, I erect a wall before it, guarding it. The finest cord connects it to the darkness inside me, to that deep pool of power within, and I hold fast as it shimmers and waits for my call.

Sadly, my body can't be compartmentalized. I can only flex and gird for Dagursson's onslaught. He strikes and slashes, and I force myself to sway under his hand. To make him think he's in charge, that he's beating me. I'll bend, but I'll never break.

He's grunting now. I hear his dissatisfaction. If he'd hoped I'd shout and cry and shriek, I'm determined to disappoint.

"You're a strong one." He throws down his knife with a clatter. "This is too blunt." Once again he's rifling through his tools, and my rational mind clings to the sound. I could let go and slip away, but it's not in me to give up. I have to hold on. "Perhaps something with a hook will help crack the stubborn bone," he mutters.

There's a knock at the door, and for the briefest second, it shatters the energy in the room. It's what I needed.

A rush of blood prickles through my brain. It's coursing again, bringing oxygen and strength. Clarifying my thoughts. I crane my neck to meet his eye. "Need to break for office hours?" I manage a smile, tasting blood on my teeth.

"I see I've yet to beat the impertinence from you." He comes to stand at my shoulder, too close for me to see his face.

There's another knock. I see from below how his jaw tenses. I look to the door, staring, waiting for that opportunity I know is out there.

He smacks the back of my head. "Ignore it. They'll go away."

"Please, don't let me keep you from your duties." I begin to call out, "Come—" but the vampire has grabbed my shirt and is stuffing it in my mouth.

The knob slowly turns, and the door creaks as it's tentatively pushed open. "Hello? Master Dagursson? I've been working on the irregular Norse declensions and…" A curly-haired Acari pops her head in. She spots me and widens her eyes. "Oh. Sorry. I can—"

The vampire is at the door in a blink. "Office hours are cancelled today," he says and slams it shut.

He strolls back to me. "You persist in being foolish. You must make yourself worthy if you're to bear the wings of the Blood Eagle."

Sweat drips into my eyes, and I blink hard, glaring at him. If I could spit out this shirt, I'd tell him what I thought of his bloody bird.

"Now, where were we?" He's grabbed a thin, hooked instrument, which he taps in his palm. "Ah, yes. You were going to tell me what, precisely, Alcántara has to do with this."

I raise my brow and shrug. My way of saying, *I'm gagged, dimwit.*

"You see, Ronan, you're what we call muscle. I don't quite believe that you have the capacity or the wherewithal to act alone." He pulls the shirt from my mouth, shaking it out with a look of disgust. "So, speak."

"I'm not a dog, Alrik."

"So don't speak. However you wish. I'm losing patience." He storms behind me. I have only a second to brace before he plunges the hook into my skin, wrenches it around bone, and snaps.

A loud *crack*—so wrong, so visceral—fills my skull. The sound of my bone splitting. Pain so complete it stuns me, rips through me. Shards of bone tear tender flesh from within, searing me. The heat burns, too, the feel of my blood trickling down skin that's been deadened into cold gooseflesh.

I black out for a second and come to with a gasp. I can't let go. I keep holding on for Annelise, for that elusive opportunity that still might present itself. For a moment—an absurd, ridiculous moment—I'd hoped that was her at the door. But hope is for children, and I'm no child. I'm about to be a dead man.

How will Freya react to my senseless death, to this lesson she teaches out of spite? Will she aim her sights at Annelise instead? I know Carden will be as good as his word, that he'll protect her. So why can't I just shut my eyes and let myself go into the darkness?

As I feel the blood pumping from me, I think of my sister. Tall, black-haired, lionhearted Charlotte. Will I see her again after I die? Is there an afterlife where I'll see all of them? All the people I've cared for who've been taken from me. Is Lottie watching me even now, from above, waiting to help ease my passage? She was always so fierce and determined, almost uncontrollably so. I'd have thought nothing could defeat her. Are there others? Do they look like her? Like me?

"Tell me," I say to Dagursson. The words sap the last of my energy, but before I die, I need to know. "Just tell…what happened…my family."

He considers me, theatrically tapping his chin, reveling in his triumph. "I suppose everyone should get a final wish."

The door crashes open.

He bellows, "I said no office hours."

I can no longer lift my head. I am drifting in a warm

cocoon. I hear Annelise's voice and wonder if I've died.

"I won't be long," she says. "I've just come to get Tracer Ronan."

CHAPTER NINE

Annelise bursts into the room, arms and legs pumping. I whisper her name—the mantra that's keeping me alive. She pauses to throw two quick stars—one for Dagursson's chest, one for his throat—then spins away. She's behind the table now, from where she throws another. She's a dervish. A maniac. A creature of beauty and grace.

And it won't be enough. We'll need more than throwing stars to kill Dagursson.

Moving slowly, deliberately, he puts down his tools. He paces toward her.

I find my voice and shout, "Go. Ann. He'll kill you."

She jogs backward away from the vampire—but it's away from the door. Away from escape. She shoots me a quick smirk of bravado. "You know I hate being told what to do."

She can't do this alone—I won't let her. I pull myself out from where I'd sunk deep in my subconscious, pull myself back into the moment. My body ignites with pain.

I'm electric, every cell roused to life. Each beat of my heart is a pulse of agony and fury. And fear, too—that Dagursson will tie her up and make me watch him do to her what he's been doing to me.

"Tracer Ronan, you are being quite rude," Dagursson says in a chillingly calm voice. He continues to prowl toward Ann, beckoning, "Don't go, child. I'm so very pleased you're here. We were just discussing the difference between pain and anguish. Now that you've joined us, we can more fully explore the concept."

"Acari Drew," I yell sternly. "You will get out of here. Right now." I've used my teacher's voice, and though it earns me a surprised look, she doesn't listen.

Dagursson also ignores me. The table has halted his approach, and he pauses to lean casually across from her. "How did you know Ronan and I were sharing time together?" His pose is nonchalant, but it's clear he's poised for attack.

I shuffle my feet beneath my chair, frantically jerking my shoulders from side to side, but I'm trapped like a rat. Blood runs along my arms, down my back. The acuteness of the pain is gone, pushed to some faraway place in my mind. All I know is that I must help her. Annelise must survive.

She shrugs with the brave calm that's kept her alive this long. "A little bird told me you two were hanging out."

Dagursson considers for a moment then nods. "Ah. Your little bird would be Acari Regina, come for office hours. Am I right? She's the only one who interrupted our little *tête-à-tête*."

"I don't know who you're talking about," Annelise says blandly.

The vampire gives a knowing smile. "Ever the loyal friend." He looks at me. "Is that what draws you to her? Everyone else abandoned you, but here is an Acari, weak and lonely, who cannot leave?"

Dagursson is wallowing in this strange exchange, a child getting his moment of glory. But it works for me—with time comes opportunity. "Annelise might be many things," I say, making my tone as calmly conversational as possible, "but weak isn't one of them."

"Aw, thanks, Ronan." She beams at me, and even though I know she's just playing along, for an instant I feel lit from within.

Dagursson's brow pinches. "I wonder at the connection between the two of you. I tried to warn Alcántara, but he dismissed it." He peers intently at her. "Hugo refuses to kill you, but why? What secrets do you hide?"

His eyes are roving up and down her body, and I jerk and fight against my bonds until the urumi slices deep into my belly. "Look at me instead, coward," I say, trying vainly to wrestle free. "She's not hiding anything."

But the vampire is focused now, focused only on her. "You are a key, Acari Drew, and yet I fear what door you'll unlock." His hand skims across the table, sliding like a snake toward her. "I must kill you myself, I suppose." He leans, reaching closer. "Apologies, my child. It really is such a waste. But you're simply too dangerous to live."

"And too stubborn to die," she says with a wild smile. She throws her last star, and rather than aiming for Dagursson, she's aimed for his sleeve, pinning him to the wood.

It takes him only a second to tear his arm free, but it buys her enough time to dart away yet again, dashing for a small sofa before the hearth. She leaps onto it, her small feet dashing along the back edge, and hops up to grab one of a pair of crossed fencing sabers hanging there. "I've always wanted to try one of these," she says giddily.

She's mad. And it gives me hope.

Dagursson purses his lips, the distaste clear on his face. "Young lady, there's no call for you to be racing about like a jackal." I see how he wants to fly at her, tear into her, but he merely stalks toward her, one feral cat tracking another. "We can be civilized about this."

"Civilized?" She executes a quick hop around him. "Decorum class was last semester." She's at my back now and whispers, "Just a sec," as she quickly wriggles the saber between the urumi and my body.

Coaxing Dagursson away from me has been her plan all along, and he shakes his head, walking toward us. "You children persist in trying my patience. What is it you think to accomplish with this farce?"

He's standing right over us now, and she wrenches the saber. Steel slashes my palm. She gasps, mutters, "Sorry," but a moment later the urumi uncurls from my waist and falls to the ground, coiling back up with a sharp *snap*.

I try to find my feet and rise, but instantly double over, a veil of black dropped over my vision. Every breath is an agony.

"Enough," Dagursson thunders. "I thought we'd have a pleasant discussion, but I see we must do this the hard way." He swoops behind her and pins her in his arms.

I lunge for him but stumble as I launch from my seat. My torso is on fire. "Let her go."

I'm moving in slow motion, but Dagursson only stands there, watching me as he holds her, wearing an expression of serene patience. "Are you quite recovered?" he asks me. "Because I think I'd like you to watch." He sniffs deeply, devouring her throat with his eyes. "Watch as I take my prize."

"Face me," I scream. I'm on my feet, staggering toward them, the urumi back in my hand. My physical pain is gone, all that remains is this black sea of hatred churning inside me. "Coward, look at me. Take me. You wanted me."

But he doesn't look away from her throat—his pupils are dilated now, entranced only by her. "There are cleaner ways to kill a girl," he says in a low, considering voice. He wrenches her neck back and studies it. Licks a fang. "But this will be a rare treat."

She elbows him—not nearly hard enough to hurt a vampire—but it startles him, distracts him.

"Silly girl," he growls. She curls herself closer into him as he readjusts his grip,. "That's right, come to me." A hungry smile curves his lips. He opens his mouth.

"Silly, sure." Her sleeve is tugged back. I spot a glimmer of silver in her hand. "But not stupid."

She raises her fist, swivels, and slashes.

At first I think she's missed him. She only flailed at him—a jerking motion, a quick flash of blade. Enough for a minor flesh wound, maybe. Not enough to do anything but anger him.

But Dagursson shrieks.

He lurches backward, hands cupped over his face. And then I spot the smoke drifting from between his fingers.

"Ann," I call, stumbling toward her. "Look at me. Are you okay?" She nods wordlessly, staring at Dagursson.

We're both astounded. I lean against her, fighting to suppress my pain. "What did you do?"

There's a shift in energy, a pulsing, and slowly the vampire rises, stands tall. He lowers his hands from his face. A grisly black wound runs down his cheek. It's smoldering.

His attention swings to Annelise. He's zeroed in on the weapon in her hand. "Show me your weapon." His voice is an inhuman drone, piercing my ears, reverberating in my chest. Rage has deformed his face, making him look more demon than man. "Show me, girl. What do you have?"

My reaction is instant. I insert myself in front of her. I can't raise my right hand, and so I lift the urumi in my left. "She has me."

"How quaint." He spits the words at us, then grabs a fistful of my hair, shoving my head aside to get a better look at her. "Acari, you will hand me that dagger. Give me the dagger, and I promise to be quick as I kill the boy." He gives my head a shake.

I wrench free, feeling hair tear from my scalp. I reach behind me, pushing her back. The motion sends a fresh curtain of blood spilling down my back. She sucks in a quick breath, stepping close again, and touches me tenderly above my wound. There is no parting us.

"You'll have to go through me," I say. The handle of my weapon is warm in my palm, like a living thing. An extension of me, of us.

He darts a hand out around me, snatching at her, and I crack the urumi, slashing down. The metal sings as it whips through the air toward him. I step back to twirl it up and then down again, one fluid movement. Sketching an *X* in the air, I sever the hand from his arm.

The impact shoots my broken rib deeper into my flesh, and a great sound escapes me, a battle cry that is my defiance.

As he stares at the stump of his arm, his expression of shocked disbelief twists, sharpens. It becomes one of wrath. He leaps at me, a savage, slavering, wordless thing, but I've whipped the urumi around him and snagged his chest. He staggers, and it jolts the weapon from my grip, sending a shock up my arm. Deep in my body, broken bone grazes something vital, and I stumble, too, pitching sideways and hitting his desk, sending papers flying. Blackness beckons, my vision gray and spotty.

But Annelise is completely focused. She prowls toward him—she's the one stalking now. "Looks like I've got the upper hand, Master Dag." She kicks his hand aside from where it'd fallen to the floor. "Get it? Hand?" She lunges and strikes.

This time I hear sizzling as her strange blade slices his arm, his back. She'd missed his heart, and yet he screeches—a monstrous, unearthly sound—and drops to his knees. Howling, he wrenches his body, trying to pat at his smoldering wounds. The room stinks of sulfur and rot.

She gives the knife a little toss to her hand, reseating the weapon in her palm. "Sorry, I know how you hate my jokes."

I see her blade clearly now. A long, thin dagger, beautifully crafted—it feels as old at this island.

Dagursson sees it, too. It's all he sees. "No," he whispers. "How could this be?"

"They say you Vikings like a good death." She squats and wraps an arm around him, forming a surreal tableau. Her eyes are fevered. She's a goddess of fire and rage and madness. "Ready for yours?"

Like a creature enthralled, Dagursson is frozen in place, tracking the weapon as she raises her arm, dagger aimed at his heart. He's murmuring something in a guttural language I don't recognize. It has the cadence of a prayer.

She's about to strike. There's a loud *click*. We all freeze. The sound has come from inside the wall, and it echoes, reverberating around us. It's followed by a great moaning—the low, haunting groan of wood—as one edge of Dagursson's bookcase shifts away from the wall.

A hidden passage. We are transfixed. It creaks open.

Annelise's arm is suspended in midair. Dagursson is hunched and twitching, a creature melting in acid. And me? My mouth is agape.

Because standing before us, tall and proud, is my sister. My Charlotte.

"You?" I whisper. Have I died? Is this a hallucination? My sister come to take me to the other side?

But Charlotte—bored, annoyed—looks only at Dagursson. "Do I have to do everything, Alrik?"

"Who the hell are you?" Annelise demands. She's standing now, tense with anger.

It means my sister isn't an apparition.

I can barely breathe through my pain. I find my voice between quick, panting gasps. "Could it really be you?"

A foxlike smile curves her mouth as she spots me and prowls toward me. She's in modern street clothes, looking long and sleek and gray. "Look at you, Ro. All grown up." Her eyes rove my broken body. "And I see you're still trying to kill yourself."

"You're here," I repeat, mesmerized. Then I laugh, a giddy, childish sound. "You're here."

"You know this person?" Annelise blurts. I feel her gaze burning into me but can't tear my eyes from Charlotte for fear she might disappear again.

"Yes, I'm here. I've been here. Why do you think you're still alive?" She looks back to Dagursson and sighs heavily. "Bugger all. Look at this mess. How did you manage to do this? You always were a pain, little sport."

"Help me." Dagursson moans and reaches for Lottie. "Feed me."

"You've been with Dagursson, all this time?" I try to stand upright, but my own bone stabs me from within. I bite back a cry, gritting my teeth, grasping for clarity. "I don't understand. How are you alive?"

"Alive? Not quite." Charlotte grins, baring gleaming fangs. She hisses at me. When I flinch, she breaks into bright, tinkling laughter—it's the sound of a young girl, a sound I remember. She dabs an eye. "Oh, Ro, for chrissake. Shut your mouth before you catch something in it. You look like a sodding daftie." She paces a circle around the dying vampire, huddled into a shrinking mass on the carpet. "Of course I'm alive. Do you really think I'd let some delinquent from suburban…I don't know"—she waves a hand—"wherever that girl was from…do you really think I'd let someone like *that* kill me?"

"Ronan," Annelise says sharply. I tear my eyes from my sister, and what I see kicks me in the chest. Fury but also—thrillingly—jealousy make Ann's eyes glow. "Who is this girl?"

Charlotte swivels her gaze slowly, languorously, toward Annelise, perusing her as though assessing a cut of meat. For the first time since she appeared, true fear prickles the back of my neck.

A sharp crack of a laugh escapes Lottie. "Oh! I know who *you* are. You're the girl my brother's in love with."

Annelise pins me with her eyes, part shocked, part flustered. "You're in…? She's what…?" She looks back to Char. "This is your *sister*?"

Somewhere in the back of my mind I'm relieved she chose not to address the love part of that equation.

Charlotte nods. "Can't you see the resemblance? Though I got all the brains in the family. Ronan here…he's just the troublemaker." She squats and traces the hair from Dagursson's brow. "I'll never guess how you managed this. Now I'll have to feed the old sot myself."

"What are you doing helping *Dagursson*?" I ask.

"I'm not helping anybody. Alrik here is helping *me*. I'm having him trace our lineage." She strides to the sofa, pulls off a pillow, and systematically shreds the case into strips. "I won't let you kill him, you know. He's the keeper of the lore. He knows all the genealogies. The family trees. *Our* family tree. We're of powerful stock, you and I. Descended from druids and seers, we are. But first thing's first: Lift your arms, little man," she says, standing before me once more. I do as she says, and she begins to wrap my bare chest tight. "Though I guess I can't call you 'little man' anymore, can I? You've been working out." She lightly smacks my bare chest and shoots Annelise a grin. "I'll bet you like the view, don't you?"

"I don't like that he's injured, no," Annelise says, but her cheeks have turned crimson. I lose myself for a moment, watching her, transfixed by what is a visual symphony of expressions moving across her face. She won't meet my eye.

Lottie laughs and ties off my binding with a sharp tug, slamming me back into reality.

I shoot her a glare. "Easy, Char."

"Don't be a baby." She pats my cheek. "Just think how bad this would be if you were a normal man. But you're not normal, Ronan." Her hands slide to my shoulders, gripping tightly. "And you're not just a Tracer, either. You're a pure-blooded Celt."

She wanders back to Dagursson, standing over him. We all study him—he's twitching now, a sizzling, melting mass on the floor, barely alive. "Bloody hell," she mutters, rolling up her sleeves. "I'll stain my shirt."

"How did you even get this way?" I ask, dumbfounded.

"I told you. He turned me."

"You just…asked him?"

"Don't be daft. I tricked him." She nudges the vampire with a toe of her pointed boots. "Old boys like Dag here think females are dumb. That we should be seen and not heard, all that nonsense. I like to think I enlightened him."

"How?" Annelise asks, sounding a bit in awe.

Lottie hitches a thumb my way. "You know how he's got his special talent? Well, I have talents, too." She sees my surprise and laughs. "That's right, Ro. I never told you. *You're* the idiot who tells everyone everything. I never told anyone. I convinced Alrik to turn me, and then, uh-oh, guess who's the strong one now?" She laughs, and she might as well have been giving a football replay for all her casual calm. "He might be a Viking, but we've got the old blood. The Celts were here first, Ronan. Who else do you think made the first vampire, if not the Druids? We're way more powerful than any Viking or Spaniard or whatever." She waves it away. "We're wasting time. We need to get out of here before this stench travels and his lackeys come running. I'm so not in the mood."

Charlotte is alive, I'm injured, and Annelise is watching me with an expression that says she's not forgotten the whole I'm-in-love-with-her bit. Assassination can wait.

"Fine." I reach out my hand, and Ann's fingers twine

through mine. My heart swells, my eyes only for her as I say, "Let's get out of here."

Charlotte shoulders between us with a smirk. "Sorry, little brother. Where we're going, there's no room for baggage."

"Baggage?" Annelise says sharply.

"Ann is no baggage," I say calmly. I know both women, and I'd like to stop this whole standoff before it snowballs out of control.

Charlotte sighs. "Spare me the love-struck drama. If you need the girl to live, fine. But I'm no babysitter. Your girl stays here." She squats beside Dagursson. "I'll have enough drama sorting this mess out."

My eyes are glued to Annelise as I say, "I'm not going anywhere without her."

"I've had quite enough of that, Ro. Now just shut up and—"

"You don't order me around. I'm not twelve anymore, Lottie."

"Do *not* call me that." She scowls and shudders. "Fine, you're"—she pauses briefly—"nineteen now, is it?" She hoists Dagursson to his feet, looking at me with an expectant look. "Well? Are you going to help me with this or not?"

"What are you doing?"

She frowns, surprised that I'm not following her unthinkingly. "Is that any way to show me you've missed me?"

"Missed you? I mourned you for years, Char. Bloody hell. I was gutted. You could've given me a sign you were alive."

"Must we do this now?" She drops Alrik, and he grunts as he hits the ground like a sack of dead weight. "I didn't tell you because I didn't trust you to not give me away. I have plans, Ronan. Big plans." She reaches out and pinches my chin. "Don't worry. They involve you, too."

Unease prickles the back of my neck. "What plans?"

She comes to stand toe-to-toe with me, as though we're facing off. In her boots, she's tall enough to look me straight in the eye. "Did you know Tracers can be Vampire?"

I've no clue where she's going with this. I meet her gaze unwaveringly. "Tracers don't survive the transition. We're saturated with enough power already."

"Some Tracers live through it." She jabs her thumb Annelise's way. "Her Carden did."

Ann gasps. "Carden was a Tracer?"

"Fine," I say, not eager to bring *him* into this. "Some survive. A few. *Very* few."

"Ah, but those who do"—she beams—"they're not just regular vampires. Between your abilities as Tracer and our bloodline?" She looks to the sky, smiling and sucking in a breath as though lost for words. "The possibilities, Ro. Think about it. You'd be the strongest. The most powerful."

"If I survived."

"Don't be such a little wanker. You'd live. You know you would."

She's right. I'm strong—I probably would survive. In my darkest hours, I've entertained the notion. To become Vampire. It's a fate both repellant and enticing.

"Carden was a Tracer?" Annelise repeats, and I can't read the subtext in her voice. Do I hear grief for what he used to be? Or is she attracted to the possibility of ultimate power?

"Oh, aye," Lottie says. "It's why the Directorate won't kill him. McCloud is too strong, with too much potential. They think they can harness it. And anyway, I don't think there's any one vampire who *could* kill him."

Annelise's eyes go wide. "Carden is that powerful?"

"We should go," I say abruptly, "*all* of us. As fascinating as this is, we should discuss it somewhere safer." I scoop the urumi from where it'd fallen beneath the table.

Lottie's eyebrows snap together. "Hey, that's mine." She

snatches it from me and hooks it at her waist. "I've been looking for this." She gives me an impatient nod. "Come on, then, let's get Alrik on his feet."

"On his feet? The only place I'll see Alrik Dagursson is in his grave."

Annelise gapes. "You're taking Dag? You have got to be kidding me." She's standing by my side now—she's *on* my side.

Charlotte's features crystallize, smoothing like ice. For the first time, I see her truly, as the vampire she's become, radiating an unearthly essence that goes deeper than fangs. Her eyes narrow on Annelise. "I don't kid."

"No? Then I guess you're just a lunatic, because it's insane to drag a bleeding, dying vampire—check that—*Directorate* vampire out of here."

"The only crazy one here is my little brother for wanting you around." Charlotte stalks toward Annelise, wraps her hands around her neck, and backs her into the wall.

I jump up, broken rib forgotten. "Get your hands off her."

"Oh, sod off, Ro." Lottie sneers and shoves Ann away. "You mortals never could control yourselves."

Annelise stands tall, pulling her shoulders back—it's a stance I know well, and my every muscle flexes. "Easy," I murmur to her. I'm on alert, ready to intervene.

But Ann ignores me. "Maybe my math is off," she says tartly, "but weren't you a mortal yourself, like, I don't know, a couple years ago?" She waves her fingers and skips backward from Charlotte, intoning in a low, mocking voice, "Oh, ancient one."

"Bloody hell," I mumble, edging between the two. "Ladies, we have bigger concerns just now." A distant slamming door proves my point. "Like *that*, aye? So let's take this elsewhere, shall we?"

"I've got one more thing to do." Annelise drops to her

knees beside Dagursson. He's moaning now, legs writhing, skin bubbling. "Time to say good-bye to your buddy, Lottie."

"You will not kill him," Charlotte orders.

But Annelise doesn't budge. "You're a Viking," she says to Alrik, "so I guess I need to be bidding you something like 'Godspeed,' right?"

Outrage and disbelief distort my sister's usually flawless features. Even when she was merely human, nobody—*nobody*—disregarded her like this. She storms toward Annelise, but I grab her arm to stop her.

"Wait," I command, summoning a pulse of power from so deep, it turns my stomach.

Charlotte stops and sucks in a startled breath. Her eyes are wild, and she pins them on me. "Get. Off. Me."

I give her an even smile. "We're adults now, Charlotte. Let's discuss it that way."

Charlotte's voice is steel as she slowly tells me, "Don't do your little tricks on me. Tell that girl to get up this instant. I'll kill her, Ronan. I swear I will. Unless she gets up right now."

My sister tries to jerk away, but I don't let go.

Annelise raises her arm. That strange dagger is in her hand again. She tilts it so it catches the light. "I know I'm supposed to aim for the heart, but from the looks of your other cuts, I bet I don't even need to aim with this thing."

"What are you doing?" Lottie shrieks. "What is that blade?" she demands of me.

I shrug. "That thing was news to me."

Annelise flashes my sister a challenging smile. "It's like you said, *Lottie*. We mortals are so impulsive." And then she sweeps her arm down in a graceful arc. She is power and determination and beauty as she plunges that strange, slim dagger deep into Dagursson's heart. His corpse erupts, his body roiling, smoking, hissing. It's the sizzle of molten steel dropped in cold water. Annelise gives me an exaggeratedly apologetic look. "I guess I really need to work on my self-control."

I don't think it's possible to love her more than I do in this moment.

I'm distracted, and Charlotte manages to break free of my grip. "You just killed the only link to our family," she screeches, her gaze skittering nervously between Ann and me. I see how she wants to leap on Annelise, but for the first time ever, I see fear in my sister's eyes. She points at Ann. "Who is she? Who is she, *really*?"

Annelise killed a vampire—a powerful, ancient one—which makes her an unknown quantity. Ann is a variable—and with that weapon in her possession, she's a dangerous one.

"Who is she?" I say, repeating her words. "Who are *you*, Charlotte?"

The curtain of her black hair sweeps into her face as she swings to look at me. "I am your blood kin, and you should honor that." My sister is raving, fangs bared, her face a mask of wrath and retribution.

"What did Dagursson do to you? What have you turned into?"

"I've always been me," she says in a voice slow and seething. "Little Ronan, you were a child when I left. You didn't know me. You'll never know me. Just like you'll never know this girl." Disgust twists her mouth as she scans Annelise from head to toe. "She wasn't even born here. Who is this girl that she's more important than your family?"

"Annelise *is* my family."

"No, you've lost our connection to them. If you don't come with me, you lose me, too."

"I won't leave her. I won't leave Annelise. Not like this."

"You and I, we can be more powerful than any girl."

For years, Charlotte was my reason for living. The desire to avenge her death was the only thing that got me to place my feet on the floor every morning. But no more. I'm living for something else now—someone else. Nothing is more powerful to me than this feeling I carry for Annelise.

"Go."

CHAPTER TEN

Somehow Annelise and I have made it to my secret spot, a lookout nestled in the dunes. Perched above the beach and below the path, we are hidden, and yet I feel more exposed than I ever have before. She knows too much, has seen too much. She's witnessed me at my most vulnerable. She suspects I love her—how could she not?—and there's no going back from that.

I shift, and the movement aggravates my injury. I heal quickly, but I seek the pain now, test its limits. It reminds me I'm more than just this churning frustration and unease. More than this consuming desire.

"You okay?" she asks quietly.

I dare to look at her. She sits so close. The waxing moon has painted silver outlines along her nose, her cheekbone, the upper curve of her lip. I cut my eyes away, out to the water. "Aye," I say in a rasp. "Thanks to you."

She didn't just save my life; she gave me a new one. Before Annelise came into my world, I was driven only by hatred, by the desire to have my revenge, and if it killed me in the process, then so be it. But now? Now I have hope. I still crave vengeance, but it's because of what I might claim afterward: a life shared with her.

But do I tell her this? Even if I tried, how would I?

The feelings are too much, so I smother them beneath a half-smile, adding, "Though, I do wonder what took you so long to show up." It's something she'd do, using humor to conceal emotion.

"You're welcome." She leans close and nudges my side. At the touch of her body, I am unmanned. My breath catches, but she must think it's from the pain because she quickly says, "Oh jeez, I'm sorry. How do you feel?" Before I can reply, she's hopped onto her knees and is at my back. "May I?"

Her hands are on the hem of my sweater. I don't know what she's about to do, but I won't stop her. I give a tight nod.

She pulls up both my sweater and shirt. The night air is cold enough, but my skin feels fevered, and a shiver ripples up my body.

"Oh, Ronan." She traces the outline of my injury—the Blood Eagle she saved me from. "That must've *hurt*."

Every muscle in my body tenses. Her tender fingers on my bare skin are too much to bear. "You could say that," I manage through gritted teeth.

She pulls everything back into place and squeezes my shoulder. Her movements are stiffer than before. Does she sense this tension too? "That Dag was such a sicko. I don't suppose he used antiseptic on those creepy tools of his, either. Like, sterilize them, or something." She settles once more beside me, and I feel the agitation rippling off her body. She's wound up and ready to chatter. Is the nervous energy because she wants to be near me or because she'd rather be near *him*?

"Good thing I'm a Tracer," I say. Not a vampire. I look at her, willing her to catch the unspoken thought in the intensity of my gaze.

But she only nods. "And then there's that whole full-blooded Druid thing…" She tapers off. Wrapping her arms around her knees, she seems to curl into herself, beneath a cloak of self-consciousness. She'd be thinking of my sister—I know I am.

"Aye," I say, not wanting her to think she's said anything wrong, "there's that."

"Are you going to go after her?"

I sigh. "Eventually. I mean, yes. Soon." There are other things foremost on my mind at the moment.

"You must be happy. That she's alive, I mean."

"Of course. But…" I'm not sure how I'm feeling. Am I empty? Relieved? Maybe even a little afraid? "Discovering Lottie alive? I'd have thought I'd feel immeasurable joy. But I find I'm…anxious. She's smart, my sister. And she's up to something. She's a mystery."

"And you're afraid of the answer?"

I nod. She's got it exactly. "Something like that, yes."

Annelise has an intent look on her face, as though she might say something meaningful or personal. At the moment, I can't bear either. Lightening my tone, I say, "Enough about me. What about you, you wee dervish? 'Who's got the upper hand now?'" I laugh, and it's not entirely fabricated. "You're too much. But truly, what were you thinking, bursting in like that? You could've been killed." I shake my head in genuine wonder. "I'm amazed you *weren't* killed."

"When Regina found me and told me what was going down"—she shrugs—"I knew right away what you were doing. I thought I could help you. Maybe even kill Dagursson myself. It was okay—I'm stronger than you think. And I'd just fed—"

"Must you remind me?" My voice comes out sharper than I intended. But she was going to tell me how she'd just fed from Carden. Vampire blood, particularly when consumed hot and pulsing from the source, makes one powerful. Their bond had been an accident, but now that they share one, it's made her stronger. Stronger is a good thing. So why does it feel so dismal? "I get that you're bonded to him. I get that you're stronger. I get that."

I have to turn away and gaze north along the shore instead. She fed from Carden, from his veins. Veins I'd like to cut, bleeding him out until I'm the one who gives Annelise what she needs. Until it's me, not him, who provides the source of her strength.

"Don't blame me," she says gently. Her finger is light and cool under my chin. She draws my face to look at her. "I'd do whatever it takes to save your life. I can't lose you, Ronan."

I pull away. "Because you like toying with me?"

She hesitates—and it cuts deeper than any swordplay Dagursson could devise. "That's not what I'm saying."

"Then what are you saying, Ann?" *Say it. Say you want him and not me. Or say you belong to me only. Just say something.*

But she's silent.

I stare down at the waves, wanting this to be done, wishing I could just fling myself over the cliff into the sea's brutal embrace. "I don't need your mercy."

"What does that mean? That's not it at all." She runs her fingers through her hair, cradling her head in her hand. "You're…you're confusing me."

"What's confusing?" I twist to face her, cupping her chin in my hand. The move jars my injury, but I don't care. I lean closer, my eyes glued to her mouth, and burn where my body touches hers. "Do you not want me to touch you?" I whisper. "It seems I must ask outright. But I need to know, Ann. Do you want this?"

Her breath catches. "I'm bonded to Carden."

"Enough with the reminders. Trust me, your bond is all I think about. Is that what you *want*? Say the word, and I'll leave. I'll disappear forever."

"No." Her voice is pained. "I don't want you to leave. Not at all. I want you here. All the time. That's what confuses me."

I exhale, my lungs functioning again. "That's all I need to know."

"What are we going to do?"

"I'll think of something."

"But Carden…. He'll kill you."

"Not necessarily." My head snaps up with an idea. "We have something he needs."

She raises her brows in question. "You mean me?"

"No, you he *wants*. But that dagger… May I see it?"

"Please." She gives me a grateful nod and unzips her jacket. "Honestly, it's kind of freaking me out. I feel like it's alive or something." She reaches into a hidden pocket and pulls out the unusual weapon, holding it up like a torch.

Dagursson had known it on sight, and looking closer, it's familiar to me, too. I'd seen such a thing myself…on Freya's hip. "Jesus, Ann." I meet her eye, deadly serious. "Where did you get that?"

Her sheepish expression is something I recognize, and I brace for the explanation. "Ann?" I prompt.

"I stole it," she says finally, adding in a rush, "when I broke into the keep."

"You took it from the keep?" I ask sharply.

She doesn't pause, just rattles on, "That woman vampire I told you about, Sonja, she used it. She said it's called the misericordia. It's a ceremonial thing. Nobody saw me. Nobody knows I have it. Are you angry with me? Don't be angry."

I shake my head. "No, you mad, wild girl. I'm just happy you found your way back out again." I hold out my hand for it. "May I?" I take it from her carefully, tilting it to catch the light of the moon. It's a beautiful object—slim, elegant, and very, very old. "They'd kill you if they found this in your possession."

"I've kind of figured that out." She looks nervous—it's a sight I don't often see. "Did you see what it did to Dagursson? Will they be able to sense that I have it?" Her hands are raised, as if she's handed off the hot potato and now doesn't want it back. "I don't know if I should hide it or what to do with it. I'm seriously tempted just to throw the thing in the ocean."

"What you do is let me keep it." I don't need to think about it; I simply roll up my sleeve and slide it into one of the leather straps I use to conceal my stakes.

"What are you doing?" She grabs me. "That'll get *you* killed."

My arm automatically flexes at her touch. "Not if nobody finds it."

"But by now they know someone broke in. They know someone took it. What if they find it on you—they'll think it was you."

"And I'll let them." I look hard into her eyes. When she begins to protest, I cut her off, insisting, "They can't know it was you. They'll kill you for it. Quickly and without warning."

She's silent. The moment hangs. I'm the first to pull away, adjusting my sweater back into place. I wait a moment then sweep the back of my finger down her cheek. "Ann? Are we agreed?"

She's unable to look away from the spot on my sleeve where the dagger is hiding. "It scares me. That thing has power. Sonja—the vampire—she uses it to cut the girls. Then they…the boys…" She falters.

"Don't," I say, stopping her, pulling her close. I have some idea what happens in the vampires' castle—I don't need to hear it. "I can just imagine what it is those wee bastards do."

I pull away, realizing what I need to say. "You can't

mention this to Carden," I tell her, praying it's not the thing that makes me lose her.

Her eyes sharpen. "What? Why?"

"Because he's a vampire," I explain, "and this thing"—I make a fist, feeling the dagger cut into my forearm—"this is the thing that can make or kill them."

"But he's on our side."

"Even so." I can't explain why, but until I know Carden's true motivations, I don't trust him. "Just don't. Just for now. Please?"

"I don't like having secrets," she says.

"Aye, and it's what I love about you." The words are out of my mouth before I have a chance to check them. I stiffen, hold, and like that, my decision is made. This is the moment I'd normally pull away. This time, I don't. I've said the words, and now I let down my walls and allow myself to feel them.

I pull her close, tucking her under my arm. Warmth fills me. Slowly, it begins to vibrate between us. Heat builds until she gives a small shiver in my arms.

She peers up at me. "Are you using your special voodoo touch? Like, 'Wonder Twin powers activate?'"

"Wonder whats?"

"Never mind. It's a cartoon thing. You know, American television?" Nervously, she waves it away. "Not your thing."

I wish it were. I wish lazy mornings, Sunday crosswords, and inane television shows were my thing.

"No," I say quietly, "no powers. Just me. Just my hands. Nothing more."

That silences her. She feels it, too, this connection.

"I'm scared, Ronan. I can't be with you. But..."

"But I can't be without you either," I finish, speaking for both of us.

"But Carden," she says.

"I know." It's dangerous, this thing between us. Carden's

a laid-back fellow, but if he knew the depths of my feelings, he'd kill me. I need him to part from Annelise, and he must believe he's come to the conclusion on his own. For now, he thinks I'm weak, and for now I'll let him.

"He said he found my mother," she says.

"Your mother?" I realize I'm gaping. I'd seen the photo of her mother—I'd stolen it back for her. When Annelise had told me she was dead, I'd believed her.

"She's been alive all this time." She shrugs, taking a moment to tamp down the emotion I hear rising in her throat. "All this time, she let me live with…with that man. He said he was my dad, but who knows? I mean, somebody must know. Somehow Carden found her."

So that was where Carden had been. For much of the semester, he was simply gone. I just assumed he was on a mission for Freya, though at the time, I'd thought he was being selfish, leaving Annelise to suffer without feeding from him. I'd watched as she weakened, did what I could to help her. And now, to find out he'd been doing something—something selfless—with thoughts only for her… It disturbed me in ways I didn't want to think about. "That was kind of him," I say tightly.

She remains nestled against my chest, and after a moment, I feel her give a small nod. "I don't know what to think anymore. Did Carden know all along that she was alive? What else does he know that he's not telling me?"

"Don't blame him," I say, even though I can't believe I'm about to defend him. "I think on this island we don't always understand the meaning of what it is we do know."

"What are we going to do?"

I take a deep breath. She's not going to like what I have to say. "You'll do nothing. You'll stay here, and you'll keep your head down and go to your classes. Without me here you'll have a chance to see what it is you truly feel for McCloud."

She pulls away. "Wait, what? Where will you be?" Are those tears in her eyes, or is it just the moonlight?

I squeeze her closer. "I have to leave," I tell her. "I won't be far."

"No." She gives my chest a shove while still holding tight. "I hate that you guys keep leaving me."

"I'll never leave you. Not for good."

"What if I need you?"

"You'd best need me." I stroke her hair, tilting her head and coaxing her eyes to mine. "We're not done, Annelise Drew. I will come back for you. But this is the only way. They know someone stole the dagger. If I leave, it'll take all eyes off you. You won't have to look over your shoulder. They'll link my absence, and the death of Dagursson, with the stolen dagger. They'll assume I stole it and fled. It'll create chaos. Give you your opportunity."

"My opportunity to what?"

"To see if Emma lives."

She peers at me like she's only now seeing me. For the first time ever, she's speechless.

I smile, despite myself. "I know you well, Annelise Drew."

Light dances in her eyes. Perhaps she's longed to be seen as much as I have. "It's what you love about me?" she asks playfully.

"Tease." I cup her cheek. I want to kiss her, and she looks like she'll let me, but I need to make sure of one more thing. I comb my fingers back and through her hair, cradling her head, keeping her eyes locked on mine. "But listen to me," I say, growing serious. "In this, you must trust Carden. He might be my rival, but he does care for you—more deeply than I'd like to admit. Trust him to help you. Keep what you know about the dagger to yourself, but you must seek his help if you're going to get out of there alive. Whatever you do, don't go back into that castle alone."

She reaches for my hand, twining her fingers with mine. "I wish you didn't have to go."

"Believe me, if there were any other way, I wouldn't leave you."

And this time, I do let myself kiss her. And she allows it. In this, as in all things, she meets me halfway.

As we part, I make a silent vow. I'll come back more powerful than ever. I got Annelise into this, and I'll get her out again.

CHAPTER ELEVEN

"Tracer," a sharp voice calls, stopping me on my way back to my room.

I'm not in the mood for this. For Carden. I stop, turning as he approaches. I don't wait till he's reached me before I say, "Tell your mistress it's done. They'll find Dagursson dead, if they haven't already."

He reaches me, brow cocked in that way of his. "*My* mistress? She's your mistress, too, last I checked. And you can tell her yourself when you return to *Eilean Ban-Laoch*."

"I'm not going back."

"What nonsense is this now?"

"I won't go back."

"No, lad, she said you could pay your wee visit to the Isle of Night so long as you promised to kill Alrik. You killed him—and a fine job at that, by the way. I confess, I didn't know you had it in you. But now the job's done, and so is the visit. You have no choice but to obey."

"I'm her soldier, not her slave. I'll leave the Isle, but there's something else I need to attend to."

His eyes harden. "You'll *attend* to Freya, and tonight."

"I see you've really cozied up to her. I mean, minding

her chosen ones, delivering her messages… What else do you do for her?"

He stares me down for a prolonged moment, then simply shrugs a shoulder. "Here's a bit of advice, lad. When you find yourself in hell, you'd best hug the devil."

"And what if I'm not one for hugging? What then?"

Something clicks in his expression. "You returned for the girl, and now you do something else for her, too."

I play dumb. "The girl?" I want to hear it—I want to make him say her name.

"We share a bond, Drew and I, and I'm not letting her go. If you want her, you'll have to take her from me." He scans me up and down. "I don't know that you have it in you. Now be a good boy and return to *Eilean Ban-Laoch.*"

I don't budge. "I don't take orders from you."

"If you disobey, you've gone rogue."

"And you're going to stop me?"

"You know I could," he says with a dangerous smile.

"A threat, is it? What would Annelise think if you were to kill me? I don't imagine it'd go over too well," I say, watching as the truth of it registers. "Checkmate, McCloud. You can't convince me, and you can't kill me, either."

I slip away before he decides he doesn't care what Annelise thinks.

But I'll be back.

Read on for an excerpt from the next book in the Watchers series by Veronica Wolff.

Excerpt from Reckoning

The Watchers
Book Five

Chapter One

"You have changed my life. Given me hope." His hand traced down my side, dipped to my waist. Stroked along my hip and down my thigh. "You are light where there was only darkness."

I turned into him. We lay on my bed in the shadows. His eyes, even in the dimness of moonlight, were haunted. It was dark, and yet I could call to mind their deep green color as easily as I could the shape of my own hand. He was mortal and only a couple of years older than me, but sometimes those eyes made him seem as ancient as any vampire.

That gaze was heavy on me now. Drawn to me only.

"Ronan," I whispered.

But he was done with talking. He pulled me closer and

kissed me softly. I savored the feel of lips I could draw from memory. How long I'd studied every inch of that face, and yet so few days had passed since it'd been mine to touch.

He drew back. Those eyes, so soulful and all-seeing, remained locked on me. "Why are you with him when you should be with me?"

My throat clenched. *Carden.* My affection for the ancient Scottish vampire ran deep. The bond I shared with him infused my blood.

But this thing I felt for Ronan, it went beyond chemical. It penetrated a secret heart I didn't realize I had.

Ronan must've seen the thoughts flicker across my face because he brushed the hair from my forehead, as though he might sweep my mind clear. "Let's run away. We'll disappear. Live in some faraway place." His voice was suddenly husky with intensity.

"But I'm…"

I was…what? In love with Carden?

Was I? How was that possible when all my mind could summon was Ronan?

"I'm with Carden," I said finally. We shared a bond—a bond that might endanger me were it severed.

He pulled away completely then and rolled onto his back, leaving a Ronan-sized chill along one side of my body.

"You're with Carden because you bonded," he told me, his voice tight. "By accident. It's naught more than a chemical reaction. You might as well be bonded to a drug. It's your blood that calls for Carden." He swung that tormented gaze back to me, and it was like the tide, mysterious and powerful, drawing me more deeply to him. "But your heart? Tell me, Ann. What does your heart tell you?"

"My heart?" My heart pumped blood that was bonded to Carden. To cut that bond would be to endure the blood fever. "There's no way around it," I said finally. Desperately. "The blood fever…"

I'd been parted once before from my vampire. The physical effects were devastating.

Ronan's hand flew to my face, cupping my cheek. "The blood fever I can soothe."

The hope in his voice cracked something inside me.

"How?" Even as I said it, I knew. I took his hand in mine. "Your touch."

Ronan had the power of persuasive touch. It was what he used to convince kids like me to come to this island of death. The vampires identified us—teenaged misfits, runaways, addicts, those of us who wouldn't be missed—but it was Tracers like Ronan who traveled the world, hunting us, bringing us to the Isle of Night. Different Tracers had different strengths, and Ronan's was his touch—when he used it, it was enough to persuade anyone to do anything.

I rolled away. "Your touch could help, sure, but for how long? You'd soothe the blood fever, but eventually—"

"It could be gone forever. If you let me try." He took my arm and pulled me back into the shelter of his body. "I'm strong, Ann. Stronger than you know."

He was strong. Could he be that strong?

Before, I wouldn't have thought so. But recently I'd seen him unleash his power on a vampire. It'd almost been enough to overcome one as ancient as Master Dagursson. Might it be enough to completely sever a blood bond?

"You must let me try, at least. Think, Ann. You could be parted from him forever. Let me do this for you." His tone grew earnest then. "For once, let me use my power for good."

I'd never heard him sound so vulnerable. I'd always known Ronan despised the work he was forced to do. Increasingly, he let me in enough to see just how deeply his hatred ran.

"But how…" The words came so slowly, my mouth frozen. "How…"

I couldn't get the words out. Why was my jaw so leaden? My tongue so thick?

"Be easy," I heard. There were hands on me. Cool hands. "Be easy, lass."

I opened my eyes. I was in Carden's arms.

My pulse gave a sharp, defensive kick.

"What…?" I glanced around, trying to make sense of this.

And then my heart plummeted. Just a dream.

"Hush, dove. You were dreaming." Carden snuggled me closer and placed his palm over my heart. "Your blood races." His hand swept from my chest and down along my belly, coming to rest heavy over the very core of me. "Was it me you dreamt of?"

My cheeks burned, and I was grateful for the darkness. Slowly my heartbeat returned to normal. Still, it felt as though it was pumping air, not blood.

Guilty guilty guilty. Ronan had shocked me when he'd stolen two kisses, and apparently they were still at the forefront of my mind. The forefront of my *everything.*

He'd kissed me, and I'd kissed him back, and I could never, ever tell. I dared not even think about it. If Carden were to find out, he very well might kill him.

"You expect me to say? A girl has to maintain some mystery." I gave him a saucy smile but had to force my lips not to tremble.

His hand skimmed down and around, curling beneath my thigh, and then he swooped me atop him. "Indeed?" He returned my smile. It was wicked and roguish.

Was I imagining the distance in his eyes? Carden was of an ancient Celtic line from which he'd inherited tremendous intuitive powers. Had he sensed he wasn't the one who haunted my dreams?

I panicked as I bent down to kiss him.

Honestly, it was no great hardship.

Handsome Carden. He was as noble as any knight. Fierce as any warrior. He'd been only nineteen when he turned Vampire hundreds of years ago. His youthful body was frozen in time, and yet his heart was ancient, righteous, belonging to a hero of old.

And that heart loved me. It was intoxicating.

He kissed me back, eagerly, gruffly. There was a growl in his throat. "That's more like it, my beautiful wee firebrand."

Unable to stop an abrupt laugh, I sat up, straddling him. He'd called me "dove," "petal," "sunshine," "bonny," and once, "hen." But never "firebrand."

"Am I that much of a troublemaker?" I asked, but a fresh pang of guilt made me queasy. *If only he knew.*

"Oh, aye. In the most magnificent of ways." He threaded his fingers through my hair and pulled me back to him. The humor in his eyes was smoldering into something hotter. "And now it's time for show, not tell."

He kissed me again, but as he did, a part of my mind spun out of my control. Why had I let Ronan kiss me when I had *this*? Carden was wonderful. So why, in my dreams, did Ronan kiss me still?

Carden's mouth moved along my jaw and then whispered in my ear. "Where have you gone, sweetest one?"

He was immortal. Powerful. Impossibly so. He placed me above all others. Who wouldn't want to be with such a creature?

And yet Ronan kept a hold on me.

Which one was true? Which one was love?

For the dozenth time, I shoved such thoughts from my mind. Dreams were just that—fantasies based in unreality. Even if it was the wishful thinking of my unconscious mind, it wasn't real. And those kisses Ronan and I had shared now felt like no more than that—dreams. He hadn't even stayed afterward. He'd said he was going away, and I didn't even know to where.

But Carden was here, beneath me.

"I'm right here," I told him as I speared my fingers through his hair to pull his mouth close for another kiss.

I needed to be with Carden. This was crazy.

With Ronan, it'd been just a couple stolen moments. Carden and I had shared so much more. I adored him. He'd told me he loved me, and I believed him.

And like that I was lost to my thoughts again. Before I realized what was happening, Carden had stopped kissing me. We were laying side by side. Yet another moment lost to my overthinking. "Wait." I propped up on my elbow. "Where are you going?"

Now he was getting up. Donning his plaid.

From faraway came the distant gong of the dawn bell.

"I must hurry," he said. "And you must lie low. That pup Ronan has set the whole isle to chaos. Killing Dagursson as he did…he made a mess of it." He *tsked.*

But ultimately that'd been my mess. *I* was the one who'd killed Dagursson. In letting people believe he was the culprit, Ronan was protecting *me*.

I'd stolen the misericordia from Sonja, the ruler of *Eyja nœturinnar*, this Isle of Night. It was the rarest of weapons, a dagger that could both make and kill vampires, and I'd used it to destroy one of the most powerful vampires on this island. It was only a matter of time before Sonja realized it was gone.

At great risk to his own life, Ronan had taken the blade off my hands. He'd told me how any vampire—Carden included—would do anything to have it for their own ends. He had insisted I not tell anyone about it or the part I'd played in Dagursson's death. Seeing as Ronan had risked all to direct attention away from me, I had to honor his wishes. I'd keep our secret.

All our secrets.

Yet another secret I kept from my vampire. Yet more

guilt.

Carden sat on the bed to lace up his boots. "With Dagursson dead, there is a power vacuum."

It took me a second to follow the topic change.

"And you know how nature loves a vacuum," I joked weakly. It was all I could muster. This chat with Carden was skirting every single white lie I'd ever told. It was pretty unsettling.

Dagursson had allied with Ronan's sister, Charlotte. Charlotte, who was probably out there this minute, plotting my untimely death. She was a vampire now, and Ronan had been as shocked as I was when she'd appeared. Apparently, she was a little sassier—and a lot deadlier—than when he'd last seen her.

I tried to calm myself. "But Dag was just a weirdo etiquette teacher, right? So he'd been in charge of the scrolls—he can't have been the only vampire who's able to translate those things. How does his death change anything?"

Carden pinned me with an uncharacteristically grave look. "Don't mistake me. I dance on that Viking bastard's grave, but his death brings instability. There are those who've chosen sides, who are making their secret loyalties known."

"Secret loyalties?" Why was my face burning? Sure, I had a secret or two, but it wasn't a "secret loyalty."

"Aye, not all support Fournier," he said, referring to the headmaster of the Isle. "Perhaps not even Alcántara. And it seems some of those scrolls are missing. The pup thinks to steal the lore for himself."

This was news to me. I knew Ronan had burned a couple of Dagursson's scrolls, precious for the knowledge they held about genealogies and vampire blood lines. But had he returned to the scene of the crime to pilfer more?

"I never thought Ronan the power-hungry sort," Carden said with a shake of his head. "So what is he thinking?" He pinned a sudden look on me. "Is that pup doing an errand for you?"

"Stop calling him 'pup.'" My voice was sharper than I'd intended. I forced my next words to come out calm and even. "What kind of errand would he do for me, anyway?"

"Your mother," he said, going in a direction I hadn't expected. "Those scrolls might lead him to her."

"Could they?" I felt a familiar spike in my chest—the waning and waxing of hope and despair. "What would the scrolls have to do with my mother? They're old as dirt, and she can't be much older than forty."

"Aye, but word is, she's kept company with those who are even more ancient than I."

Carden had recognized my mother from a photo. For weeks, I'd thought he'd disappeared, but he'd actually gone in search of her. He'd found only a cold trail, but for me it was enough. Now that I knew she might be alive, my dream, above all else, was to find her.

"We could look for her," I said. "You and me." I stared at him in the dawning light. He was steadfast and affectionate. Caring and carefree. He was incredibly appealing, and I adored him. He'd been there for many of my darkest hours with that rakish smile and easy laugh. "We could run away. We'd be together. We could be happy."

The words left the taste of dust in my mouth, so much an echo of what Ronan had said to me in the dream. But I couldn't imagine either of them wanting to run away, much less with me.

I swung my legs over the side of the bed, wanting to challenge him. To actually *see* that he loved me rather than merely hear the words. "We'll leave here. Find my mother. Then run off somewhere and just...be."

His gaze became distant at the mention of my mother. All thoughts of love fled as I suddenly feared that he was hiding something about her.

"What?" Maybe my mother didn't want to see me, didn't

want to be found. I hadn't seen her since I was four. Years change a person. And why had she left in the first place? "What does that look mean? Do you know something?"

"Only that it's too soon." He scooted closer to me and spoke gently. "Things need to settle here before we make any moves. The Directorate is on alert. We couldn't leave now."

"But…if things are so unsettled, isn't it a good time to leave?" I mustered a smile, wondering what he wasn't saying.

His eyes were shuttered. "There's much to do yet. Much that keeps me here." But then, as if a light switched on inside him, his attention for me returned. "Our day will come."

Our day will come. Why did I hear something else in those words? Something that went beyond our relationship to encompass the balance of power on *Eyja nœturinnar*.

END OF EXCERPT

Did you enjoy

DARK CRAVING?

Explore all of the books in

THE WATCHERS SERIES:

ISLE OF NIGHT
VAMPIRE'S KISS
BLOOD FEVER
THE KEEP
DARK CRAVING
RECKONING

Also by Veronica Wolff

Contemporary Romance
Sierra Falls
SIERRA FALLS
TIMBER CREEK

Historical Romance
Clan MacAlpin
DEVIL'S HIGHLANDER
DEVIL'S OWN

Time Travel Romance
Highland Heroes
MASTER OF THE HIGHLANDS
SWORD OF THE HIGHLANDS
WARRIOR OF THE HIGHLANDS
LORD OF THE HIGHLANDS

Novellas
LADIES PREFER ROGUES
(with Janet Chapman, Sandra Hill and Trish Jensen)

ABOUT THE AUTHOR

Like her heroine, Veronica Wolff braved an all-girls school, traveled to far away places, and studied lots of languages. She was, however, never trained as an assassin (or so she claims). In real life, she's most often found on a beach or in the mountains in Northern California, but you can always find her online at veronicawolff.com.

Visit Veronica's Website
http://www.veronicawolff.com

Find Veronica on Facebook
http://www.facebook.com/VeronicaWolffFanPage

Follow Veronica on Twitter
http://twitter.com/veronicawolff

82806474R00078

Made in the USA
San Bernardino, CA
19 July 2018